Why Don't You Care About Animals

Read "The Joys of Motherhood"

Why Don't You Carve Other Animals

Yvonne Vera

TSAR
Toronto
1992

The publishers acknowledge generous assistance
from the Ontario Arts Council and the Canada Council.

ISBN 0-920661-24-6

TSAR Publications
P.O. Box 6996, Station A
Toronto, M5W 1X7 Canada

Cover design: Natasha Ksonzek

Contents

Crossing Boundaries

James spoke as if opening a wound, cautiously and painfully. The moment had gathered, and if he let it pass, it could not be recovered easily. But there was again the prolonged compelling silence in which they were both suspended and lost. They were in an uncomfortable rhythm of their annoyance, and of their distressing circumstances. They were separated by an irresolvable territorial struggle which was articulated in the gaps and silences netted in half-formed gestures, in half-focused glances. They each heard the future thunder messages in the air around them, and the sky opened like a calabash, pouring cleansing water through the lattices of their fear. A whip cracked above, wrapping painfully around their exiled souls. What had he spoken? What?

"There is something I would like to ask for . . . madam."

His face gave nothing away. The man spoke softly to the woman, whom he feared, and who was responsible for his fear. Why should he be so cautious? Why was it necessary for him to be humble, to beg, to ask for something that perhaps belonged to him? He stood in the doorway, blocking the humble light struggling to flow in, and the cricket sounds that came through the door seemed to issue from him. He had brought the forest through the doorway and carried the last illumination of the sun on his back.

He blocked the departing rays of the sun from her, and she was in the dull shadow, silhouetted behind her desk in the recesses of the room. His eyes, darting furtively across the room, found her red hair held by a white satin ribbon. His cap rotated nervously over his fist. Overalls, torn at the knees, hung like damp sacking around his thin legs. He did not protect his feet from the earth, and they left imprints on the uncarpeted cement floor. Would he be able to ask her?

He coughed nervously, but she did not turn her head, or show any sign that she had heard. She did not encourage him to speak, and so the silence once again engulfed them, and they were uncomfortable through its message. Within that lingering space the woman was on guard. They were on guard against themselves whom they feared.

He coughed again, aggressively.

His cough was followed by her rapid command that he should close the windows, and the door. A membrane of bitterness formed around his soul, consecrating his disguise, and propelling him to the performance of the action. The thunder had lasted only a moment, echoed by her command which hovered in the corners of the room.

He pulled the windows against the gathering darkness that sent greetings through the streaks of rain, and the sky deepened. For a brief moment, after he had closed the curtains, they were enveloped in the darkness together. The light left them both, equally.

"Should I have made my proposal then?" James thought, after he had pulled the curtains. He was afraid that she would find it easy, in the unaccusing darkness, to deal with her conscience. Their situation on this land bothered her too. However, the darkness put an oppressing hand around his mouth, and he reached for the light switch. The flood of light dissolved his courage and stole his well-prepared phrases. She had not moved, and when he sought her, his eyes again were blocked by her red hair. She sat with her elbows resting on the desk, her face held in her palms.

There was tomorrow, waiting for them both. He would ask her tomorrow, in the daytime when he came to make lunch for her.

She had littered his memory with unkind words. Mostly commands. He thought always of how it could be without the presence of these strangers on the farm–it would be as his grandfather had told him.

When he had given her light, she released the face that was caged between her fingers and moved from behind the desk to the piano where she sat with her straightened back challenging him, willing him to depart from the room. He had to wait for the rain to subside, though he was suffocated by the knowledge that she wanted him to move out of her company. She was thankful for the piano and used it to protect herself against him.

Her fingers ran rapidly over the black and white keys seeking out a tune that she vaguely remembered. The situation called for something classical that would contain her and exclude him, the native. She laboured at it, but it was difficult to accomplish. But she maintained her composure, assured that he could never judge her in these matters.

The wooden doll she had bought in the theatre souvenir shop after the ballet in London stood on a table beside the piano, reminding her of her honeymoon with Charles. The streets had been white with snow. Big trees were decked with brilliant Christmas lights but she felt herself a stranger there, among the milling crowds. The doll reminded her of that white Christmas her mother had spoken so dearly of. She pursued her memory through the booklet above the piano and chose a nursery rhyme. She was safe, encased in her childhood, watching three mice run up the clock.

While she journeyed, he sat on the cold cement floor beside the sofa and listened to her play. Her music sounded unnatural to him, and he did not like the way she studied it strenuously from her book. As the rain hit violently against the asbestos roof, he wondered how much of her own music she gathered from the commotion.

When the rain had receded his eyes left her red hair and he gratefully stepped outdoors, closing the heavy door cautiously behind him. It was a while before she noticed he had left, and then she was relieved.

Loud hard pounding sent vibrations through the ground, and the frail and burdened old man sitting at the back of the hut could feel the earth move beneath his unshod feet; the women continued preparing maize flour.

Heavy wooden pestles were thrust into the sunny air, as the women worked side by side, each with her own mortar. The sleeves of their blouses were dangling freely, swirling rapidly in whorls when they heaved their shoulders upward. Their eyes did not stray from the white grains in the mortar, except when they talked to each other.

Then, they might even pause in their work, to pursue their conversation. The two women worked in the middle of a clearing, between the encircling huts of the homestead. Between them were two sacks of maize already ground, and on two mats were several baskets filled to the brim with groundnuts, which the women were going to prepare for the evening meal, after they had the maize flour ready. To the right, under the shade of the hut and close to the wall, was a calabash of clear spring water from which the women drank each time they paused. The pot of water was covered with a small leafy branch torn from a nearby bush.

Chickens wandered freely around the homestead in search of bits to eat, scratching the dry ground frantically and releasing dusty clouds which swallowed their bodies, but when they came clucking too close to the baskets of peanuts the women shooed them away. At the back of the hut, the old man, who had been dozing, followed the aeroplane droning overhead, and cursed. He could barely see it in the failing light, and was annoyed that his eyes were not what they used to be. Sitting very still behind the hut, the old man heard the women laugh, then their voices were abruptly muted by the pounding pestles. When the women were not talking, the ground resonated with their labour.

His legs now infirm, the old man remembered the migration of his people from one part of the country to the other, a forced movement across the land which symbolized the loss of their link with the soil, a journey that was a revoking of their connectedness, their belonging. Told that the land they were living on now belonged to a settler, the village had to either agree to work on the land as labourers or move to a new area that had been put aside for black people.

His father had been angry, and the old man remembered him storming in and out of the house, angered by a sense of helplessness. He would rather move than work for these criminals, but it was difficult to leave the earth where all of his ancestors had been buried, where all the culture, history and religion was contained. Was it not obvious that they were being moved to the poorest land in the country? What could they grow there? They had torn themselves away, their cattle raising large waves of dust ahead of them. Reclining contemplatively against the mud wall, the old man could see the women's elongated shadows touching the rounded shadow of the hut.

"The children should be arriving soon," MaMoyo said, in between heavy breathing.

4

"I think they are getting their school reports today. I hope Maria does well. It would be good for them to get an education," MaSibanda answered.

"Fadzai did not tell me that she is getting her school report. That makes me rather worried, does it mean she knows she did not do well?" The news of the reports made her uneasy, as she was anxious that her daughter should learn. At the back of the hut, the old man cursed.

"My father did not allow any of us girls to go to school. 'Why waste money on a girl?' he would argue. I think he just hated the idea of reading books. He would ask, after you had finished reading, 'What have you produced? Show me what you have produced!' And when he met you on your way from school he would mock, 'Where is your load? What did you carry home having been away all day?' "

[margin note: It needs to be tangible — fill your tummy]

MaSibanda laughed freely, surprised that this once hateful memory of her father would suddenly amuse her.

"My father wanted all of us to go to school, to learn the white man's secret. But he never had enough money, what with the high taxes that he had to pay on the land. So when it came to making a choice he sent the boys to school."

That had been a long journey, the old man thought. Moments passed through his head, of his youthful face, held protectively between his mother's gentle hands. He must have been at least seven when they made their harsh departure, asked overnight to become strangers to their land.

He remembered that his mother had carried him some of the way, though she was heavy with the child she was expecting, and she also supported a heavy load on her head. Most of the journey was no longer distinct in his memory, and he could not recall how many days they had travelled, or where they had spent the nights.

[margin note: Burden of ?]

Forgetting lightened the pain of their expulsion. Sometimes details surfaced effortlessly in his mind, but he could no longer discriminate between what he had experienced and what he had made up. He clearly remembered his father, whose anger could not be suppressed as he resisted each humiliating step that moved him in a direction away from his village. Some vision of his father had vanished with that degrading experience, and he again heard the planes drone overhead. The sweltering heat sent exasperating trickles of water down his neck.

[margin note: Feelings of anger / loss]

The women's laughter broke the pounding, and the old man heard

5

them resume their animated talk, about their children who were late from school, and about their life on the farm.

"It is difficult to be a woman in these times. If my daughter can get an education, she will not have to live this hard life that I have endured. She can walk away from pain." MaMoyo was confident that, given the static nature of traditions, the only escape was into the white man's world. MaSibanda, though she sent her children to school, did not always agree that the solution lay with the new education. She felt that their condition on the farm was a daily trial, and to embrace more of the culture of those who kept them subservient was hard to accept. She chose not to answer her and resumed her steady pounding.

The old man felt weighed down by the conversation of the women, which crept round the hut to where he sat, but was powerless to affect what they thought. His whole life seemed to have been a confirmation of feebleness, and it pained him to recollect. After they had reached their destination, weighed down with grave regrets and luggage, they had settled on the dry barren landscape on the edges of another settler's farm. Other families had already arrived from other parts of the country and so they all became sojourners together. The land was unlike the lush welcoming valley they had known but was spotted everywhere with curious outcrops of isolated rock, and amid the dry grass were sudden thickets of thorny bush which gave the place a desolate character. There was nothing for the exiled spirit to cling to but the grey impoverished soil. Nothing was friendly, nothing welcomed them.

The old man's first experience of the land had been unsettling. He remembered that he had gone to herd the goats, feeling dismayed, helpless, and afraid.

Cranes had landed with gentle but spindly legs among the grasses, and his heart pounded at this unexpected manifestation of another life. In the deathly stillness of the landscape, the birds moved in long quivering strides.

He had heard the cawing of crows gliding from the branch of one tree to another, looking for carrion. Anthills broke in profusion from behind every bushy covering. He kicked mercilessly at the mounds of red earth.

The children broke into the yard with loud cries of their success, skipping indifferently over the baskets full of peanuts that were waiting to be shelled, their faces beaming with excitement and pride. They

They
had done well at the end of the school term, and were now able to read and write their names.

The mothers stopped pounding the maize, casting their eyes searchingly over the reports, which they could hardly read. Soon they were satisfied with the good tidings, and sent the girls into the cooking hut, where they found some bread to eat. The old man, hearing the joyful sounds emanate from the yard, felt a confusing anger that he could not restrain. He had lost the children. He had lost the fight. A lizard circled around him, nodded its head, then skirted into the thatching.

The women had again resumed their industrious work, and the news that the children had brought from school fueled their zeal. They sang as they pounded, as though unexpectedly released from some anguish. They sang about the dream of Mungoshi, the founder of their clan:

MaSibanda our kindness shall be our death . . .
MaDube our kindness shall be our death . . .
MaMoyo our kindness shall be our death . . .

The two women sang energetically, substituting in the song the different names of the women that they knew, till their song had circled the whole village, and touched all the women and the men. They laboured tirelessly, moving their bodies between dream and reality. When they had reached the pounding end of Mungoshi's dream, they had enough maize meal to last them the rest of the week.

While the women cleaned their mortar and pestles, the old man remained concealed in his degradation, remembering how hard it had been for all of his family after the migration. They had no choice but to work on various farms around the area, competing for work with migrant labourers who arrived from as far away as Nyasaland. They picked cotton on some of the plantations, and were paid by the bag at a miserly rate. The old man was about ten then, and had thought it fun at first to pick the delicate cotton buds, which would be turned eventually into cloth. Soon he realized the work was tiring, and that the few shillings they were given at the end of the day were not enough to cover their expenses.

The land on which the farms stood was the only place in the area which could support any kind of life. Why had they been told the land was reserved for them when in fact they were being sent here to work?

7

So yes what difference did it bring to leave their homeland? why the exile then?

They might as well have stayed on their ancestral lands and worked there.

Later, when he was about twenty, he met a girl whose family lived as squatters on one of the farms. He had married her, and moved in with her family. They had borne three boys who even today continued living as squatters on the same farm. The generation that owned the farm changed, but the forms of servitude did not alter for his family.

The old man listened to his daughters-in-law talk about James, his eldest son, whom they expected to arrive soon from the farmhouse. The old man's mind could not let go of the thorns and cactus that populated the dry cracking terrain of his boyhood.

The exiled soul insists on finding a connection between moments and histories, on securing a promise from the future that there shall be compensation. The banished wanderer insists on narrating, and on situating solutions that have been evaded by the past. Caught between memory and dreaming, the hopeful exile weaves a comforting performance out of a tale of agony.

"I was foolish not to ask her."

James walked through the wet arches of maize leaves, and through a short path that led to the huts beyond the fields, to the borders of the plantation. Under the brooding sky everything had darkened into shadow and silence. His head throbbed as if he had emerged from a cruel sunlight. His family were squatters and did not pay taxes for the land that was allocated for their use, except by labour provided for the farm. They lived precariously along the fringes of the land, their souls barren of hope, and their vitality sapped by alienating labour.

Unlike his father's family, which had chosen to leave when confronted with the dire alternatives provided by the settler, his grandmother's family had chosen to stay. They had already witnessed the disappointment of the large numbers of people who had been brought from other parts of the country to be resettled among them. Their memories, located in secret places all over the land, and their ancestors buried in the land, protected them here.

The memory of the generations that had been sustained by the land made them whole, brought peace to their troubled hearts. There was no word for squatters in their language, but when they had to go to the Baas and register the birth of each child in a big heavy book, they understood that they had become strangers to the land. They had been asked to forget their ancestors, who were buried on this land.

"Tomorrow I shall speak to her, before the Baas comes from the city."

His resolution fixed, he moved into the hut in which the cooking fire in the middle of the hearth burned a dying welcome, and settled himself on a large goatskin spread on the dung-treated floors.

MaMoyo sat in the hut tending the fire. Each day while James worked on the farm she ran the home. She was eager with news that their daughter had done well at school, and of his brother's daughter, who had also done well. The two older children were already rolled in a blanket, asleep beside the fire where the warmth reached them easily.

Often MaMoyo swore she would never work on the farm, except on the plot of land that was allotted her. If she met the Madam on her way from the stream, she would not stop to talk to her. Often she cursed the earth that had betrayed them by supporting the unkind feet of strangers. It could not be helped that her husband had to work on the farm, as also his brother's family in the next hut, and his youngest brother, and all their family.

It was the youngest brother whose life they were preparing.

"Did you ask for the land, James?"

She did not need an answer, seeing his displeased face. What was Moses going to do without land on which to grow crops and support his newly acquired wife? As in most farms belonging to the settlers, half the land on this plantation lay fallow, unused. Only parts of it were cultivated, and sometimes a year might go by with nothing at all being planted. Even those who engaged in intensive farming left a lot of their land sparsely used. But they hung on to the land, adding to their wealth, denying access to those who really needed it.

James wanted a tiny fraction of fallow land for his brother. Along the borders of the land were signs hung on posts that warned against trespassing. James had the strange sensation that the flame was dying with him, that he was trapped in its ambience, but he knew that only his anger was real and that he would fight it.

Nora and her husband did not agree about keeping squatters on the land, and about their continued life on the farm.

Nora Jones had grown up on a farm where her father grew tobacco. She had met Charles at a tobacco auction, while doing business for her father. When her father died, a year after she met Charles, she had sold the farm and married. Nora's mother had died when Nora was in her teens.

Nora's mother had abhorred the relentlessly hot African climate, but her husband had insisted on their staying on. After all, they had land here, and prosperity, they could never have that in England. In Africa they could have as many servants as they chose. There was no reason why they should not stay. Nora's father heard only his own voice, trusted only his own beliefs.

Mrs Jones spoke often of her England, of the coastal village where she had grown up, and the fair she visited regularly in the summer. She spoke of very English things. A picture of herself stood on the mantel-shelf. The photograph had caught her on a swing on her fourth birthday. In the picture, a pile of snow showed behind her. She loved going to the park in winter, and she had an uncle in England who had always taken her there. The park was a lonely charming place in winter, with benches lined with snow. Africa was lonely, certainly, but it was not at all charming.

Nora pulls the curtains open and the early morning light floods into the living room, while the objects in the room leap up to her eyes; the piano, the couch, the desk. She slides the glass that constitutes most of the wall and steps gratefully into the fresh air of the veranda. Standing in her nightgown, she looks at the shimmering long green leaves of the corn, made brilliant by last night's brief rain.

Nora bathes in the light. The bricks and the asbestos of the house confine her, oppress her spirit and make her frantic with the wish to escape. The sensation of the rays on her face exalts her and wakes her, and she closes her eyes to receive the purifying light. There are many things that she wishes to escape from, that she wishes to dissolve with the bright light of the sun.

Initially, she had gathered many lamps into the house, to illumine the night. The African nights, for her, were disquietingly silent with a thick darkness. She soon found she did not like the kind of light that the lamps shed, it made her eyes tired, and filled the house with flying night insects.

Nora's husband told her to keep the curtains on her windows closed, though she wanted the light to wake her.

"The natives will see you undress."

He warned her desperately. She sensed in his voice none of the desire to defend her womanhood for himself. He was concerned only with his unquestioned domination of the native. He made it sound horrible, that a native should see her body. She began to wonder if perhaps there was indeed something unbearable about her body, something that he himself detested and thought of as he warned her of the natives. The worst threat to her dignity, to his security, that a native should see her body through the open curtains of the window, or her face in dream; her face unprepared, faceless, to meet the blank faces of the natives.

[handwritten margin note: Feelings of not being good enough; trophy wife]

Mrs Jones made a little England out of Nora, led by her own sense of self-preservation. Through her daughter, she explored the frustrated desires of her exiled ambitions. She made sure her daughter learnt ballet, listened to classical music, and read poetry. Nora's first poem, which was about the Queen, was praised by her mother. When she could play the piano, Nora was considered by her mother to be an accomplished lady. But Nora's greatest love was to paint, and she could gaze at a beautiful painting for hours, discovering worlds within it that existed only outside her lived experience. She looked at objects not always as she experienced them, but as she would like to see them painted. Reality, however, was stronger than a painted vision. Even as she stood looking at her cornfields, she felt the presence of that other life on the edge of the plantation and saw dark smoke rise into the air from the huts, which were hidden from view. Afraid to allow her thoughts to dwell on the life intimated by the smoke, she stepped back uneasily into the house, and slid the door shut firmly behind her.

On one side of the living-room wall Nora had carefully hung paintings from England that she had inherited from her mother. They were all reproductions of works by Turner. Nora was fascinated by the light in them, of the force that emanated from the mixture of colours as they merged on the canvas.

The pictures gave her a floating sense of something undecided, something incomplete and chaotic. The undisturbed surface of the water as it appeared through the fog suggested a terrifying calmness, and in some of the pictures the water did leap up like a live and ferocious thing. She liked best the pictures in which the distinct outline of objects was lost, and people became smudges and disappeared from view, moving instead like dots across an equally indistinguishable bridge. People were caught in a cloud where all is condensed in a trick

[handwritten margin note: Blurred identities like the characters described]

11

of light, in a pulse of vision. Only the light and the colour existed in a privileged purity while objects dissolved in an animated melancholy. Time dissolved from the continuous undulation of light, and Nora extracted from the canvas her safety net, an ordering of her world, and flickers of her being.

Why did Charles insist on staying on this unfriendly land?

There was much agitation in the country. Nora thought with terror of her life here, and was filled with ruthless distrust for the natives who roamed the farm. Why had James come to see her last evening? He would come back about it, she was sure of that.

There was much talk out there on the periphery of the land. The fires were observed to be burning in the huts till late into the night. What were they saying about the owners of the land? She knew they wanted the land back. Perhaps her husband would arrive soon. Two days was the longest time that Charles spent in the city, fifty kilometres away, where he had gone to buy provisions.

Charles clung to his dry contempt of the natives, whom he separated from the land itself.

"If given the land, the natives would not even know how to use it."

The labourers cultivated the land around the high maize plants with short-handled hoes, bending under the long leafy arms that extended from the stalk, and which made the skin itch when rubbed against the bare arms. As they turned the soil and collected it into protective mounds around the exposed roots of the stalk, the labourers pulled out weeds which they shook vigorously to release the soil that clung to them. Robbed of the soil from which they fed, the weeds would die. It was dark under the maize stalks which, though they had been planted in neat rows, defied these divisions and sent elongated leaves that interlinked with their neighbours. Slivers of light broke through to the bottom where the labourers were bent in their work, close to the soil. The soil offered no resistance and broke easily when one pulled out an overgrown weed.

A pile of the uprooted weeds rose into a small hill at the edges of each furrow, and the young children carried them away in their skirts, out to the edge of the field, into the early morning bright sun. Racing back to the shadows, the children found it unnecessary to bend under the stalks in the manner the adults did, and again, they did not mind the itchiness on their arms which they would soothe by diving into the cool stream that ran on one side of the plantation.

The labourers worked without signs of weariness, forgetting briefly that the land was not theirs. They loved the land, and the smell of the earth on it. They loved the promise of growing things, of time that yielded hope. The babies, released from their mother's backs, crawled along the furrows. The labourers worked without supervision, except that of James, who was related to them. It was a kind of homecoming, this communion they had with the land.

James worked on the farm and sometimes on the yard, where he tended the plants. He worked in the kitchen sometimes, when there wasn't too much work to do on the plantation. Though he had clear piercing eyes, James had a quiet look about him, and the other farmers called him a "good" black. James observed life on the farm as a temporary inconvenience, and believed that it would change. It seemed obvious to him that the anomaly of the situation called for change. The armed struggle was designed to produce such a change.

James had respect for Nora and Charles, the kind of respect that they demanded. It was always automatic to respect a white person. The couple represented for him a microcosm of the white man's struggle to feel at home on foreign soil. He saw Madam labour to absorb the landscape as she sat on her rocking chair, seeking equilibrium. Sometimes she got her paint, her brushes and her easel to assist her. She stared intensely at the sky and the trees to absorb them, her gaze enkindling a partnership with nature, imploring. Except when she walked with her dog, she withdrew from the land, as though to compensate for some trespass she had already inflicted on it.

When James went into Madam's house, he too felt he had trespassed, and that made him angry. He was forced to be obedient by the delicate doilies on the tables, the lace-covered cushions, the Queen smiling behind the door, and the piano jutting from a corner of the room. He felt his incompleteness in Madam's composure, in her swift commands. But he understood that he was incomplete because this was how she chose to deal with him. Nora dealt with James as an abstraction.

She had named him James. She claimed "James" was easier on her tongue than his native name, which she did not try to learn or understand. He held his old name between his lips whenever he encountered his new name, and in this way he expressed a power and an authority over his identity.

13

Not allowed to claim his name

To be named.
To be inscribed anew.
To be recreated.

Namelessness was what she gained for him by her alienating manner of identification. She had prepared him to be called, and reminded him of a relationship in which he was subservient.

To make the ritual complete, for indeed it was a ritual, she sent him to the colonial administrative offices where he had to "get his identity." When he returned to the farm he was Native R491766, and his right thumb had been dipped in black ink and pressed into a box marked on a large piece of paper, which he was told to carry at all times. Thus he gained his new identity, and his entrance into her world. The paper made him traceable, in case anything went missing on the farm. This was a sure way of getting loyalty out of the native, because none of them could be trusted.

James struggled with the burden of his newly acquired identity, and beseeched MaMoyo to help him, by addressing him always with his own name. But repetition and proximity exerted greater strength than ambition.

The Baas was looking for James.
The Madam was looking for James.

Shortly everyone in his family was calling him James. His new condition had been accepted, like all the other conditions that had intruded on their lives. But James was never James to himself. This secret calmed him as he worked on the land on which he was registered as a squatter. He would not complete the metamorphosis that Nora had initiated.

What is that? What did you say?
She did not know what he muttered when she addressed him.

The bush war meant disagreement, and also meant fear and distrust. Nora did not know what the Africans talked about around their fires. Her mother had kept the Africans away from her, protected her from their superstitions and their unrefined language. Nora's distrust of the Africans was also a superstition that helped her maintain her sense of difference, and of privilege.

The bush war had disrupted the calm that came with ownership of large lands and property, and the assurance she had secured with her marriage. Robbed of its solid foundation, her marriage now echoed the unsettling vibration exerted by the bush war–and she fought Charles with the need for her own survival. Circumstances created relationships.

"We should do something about the farm. Maybe we should move to the city for a while."

She dared not look at him.

"Move to the city? You know that I have never lived in the city. I would hate it there. There is no need for us to live in the city. I have told you that before. Why must you insist? Why do you bother me so?"

She had expected his frantic gesticulating, his contorted brow, his anger. That did not mean she should not insist, that she would not fight. She would speak her mind, while he ranted and raved. She was not silenced, and she did not care for his pardon, or his kindness, which she no longer expected.

"It would be safer there, for both of us. There is nothing to protect us here. There is nothing here."

He did not rise from the chair on the other side of the table where he sat, but thought a while, and she expected that he would be cruel to her. But he surprised her with his pleading, and she felt no sympathy for him, because she could not forget that he could be unkind to her.

"We have our land here, Nora. Can you not see that we have something to love here? Are you not connected to this land? Would you rather be a social lady in the city, attending tea parties?" When he finished talking she swelled with her anger, because she imagined that he laughed at her a little.

The only question that she will say No to!

"I am not talking about love, Charles. No, not love. I am concerned for our safety. The bush war, Charles. The bush war."

But he had turned away from the bush war and looked away from her, hating her. Why must she intrude on his peace? The bush war was a colossal and incurable threat to the calm that it had taken his ancestors many years to build.

Charles's grandparents had arrived in Rhodesia from South Africa. His ancestors had been in Africa for a long time, products of the Great Trek. When it bothered Charles to justify his link to this land, his sense of belonging, he talked about the Great Trek and the illustrious feats of his grandparents.

It was necessary to belong, not to feel like an intruder. Through the Great Trek his grandparents had traversed the land, bisecting its vast landscape. They had brought every kopje and every hill under their vision, heard its wild echo surround them with life, and they had named its birds and animals. They had found a language to cement their discovery, and their initiation, that was also their baptism.

Some of the migrants had not survived the crossing, but they had been sacrifices. The ordeal had strengthened their people, their race, and taught them that they could survive any situation in which their will was tested. By walking across the land, they had overcome its resistance.

They had tamed it.

Dominated it.

Claimed it.

In turn the land had given them sacred gifts. The land had a spiritual and regenerative influence, which had banished their sense of exile. Their journey was a territorial leap that released the agony of dispossession. Their claim on the African land appeared to them absolute, immutable.

"You really want to leave this farm? You are afraid. I can see how much you are afraid."

He hated her for showing her fear, and for not supporting him. She saw that he accused her with her fear, and that he recognized it as his own.

"We can buy a house in the city. The land can still belong to us, till things improve."

"I don't think we should give up, Nora. We have already given up on a lot of things, but I have worked hard on this land."

"We can come back, Charles. We can come back."

He would have believed that she meant to console him, except that she did not even raise her eyes to look at him, and shrugged her shoulders as though shaking off some responsibility that she had tired of. He read these signs with trepidation, and with pity for her, who did not understand what the land did to a man.

But why must she drag him down with her, when it was she who did not understand? Why did she ask him to behave in this cowardly way? He knew that she would mock him, after she had got her way, after he had given in to her wishes. She would regard his indulgence of her whim as a weakness, and dangle her strength over him like a trophy. He did not want to run away from a native, or give Nora power over himself. He would buy arms to protect his land, and also himself.

16

He turned away from Nora, and looked at the paintings. He did not like the paintings that Nora had brought from her mother's house, they were too English. On the adjacent wall, he had hung his own choice of paintings. He had portraits of Cecil John Rhodes, and of David Livingstone, to whom he felt the country owed its progress, and its civilization. They had been great men both, explorers, fighting disease and native ignorance as they opened up the land. These were men of courage, who annexed territory by their journeys across it.

Below these portraits he had hung a painting, a reproduction that he had bought in London, on his honeymoon with Nora. It was called "Time is a River Without Banks." The picture had appealed to his imagination, though Nora said she did not see its worth. A fish was flying over a river, a man's arm appeared on the fish's belly, playing a violin. At the right hand corner, along the bank, two lovers sat. The fish had wings and flew joyfully in a blue mist. He liked the painting because it was mysterious and fanciful, and he always found something new in it. The picture was his escape, his dreaming. He felt that its vision was complete and unified, but that there was a clear recognition in it that the perfect moment could not be eternalized. As he looked at the painting, Charles felt that he had glimpsed the height of a beautiful moment that had suddenly been corrupted, that could not be sustained. The fantasy in the painting was a witness to the collapse of an ideal.

"The trip we took on the Zambezi, did you like that? That was beautiful, Nora. Was that not beautiful?"

He broke the silence and her reverie, asking her to journey with him to a time when they were both young, and did not labour at tenderness.

"Canoeing in a river swarming with crocodiles. I was so afraid of the water. I hated the water then. But it was wonderful."

"Would you like to take that trip again... a canoe on the Zambezi? Hunting for game. I have not hunted in a long time. It would be good to go on a safari."

"It is too late to dream, Charles. It is unsafe to dream."

"We could still hunt and drive back into the city. We don't have to camp in the bush at all. Do you remember the day we saw a lion kill and eat an antelope? Camping along the Zambezi, the hyenas lurking around our camp fire? I wish for the moon, which looks strange when one sees it from the wild. The natives say it carries messages. You

is not if where it
belong?

17

used to like the moon, though of course you hated the dark."

"Think about the bush war, Charles. It is no longer safe to camp or to hunt for game. The bush is no longer yours, Charles, and we must move from a place even as half tame as this farm. Why do you continue in this way? Why do you torture yourself so with useless wishing? What happens if we are targeted? No one would know we were hurt. Do you think the squatters would help us, Charles? Do you think they would care?"

Charles could not believe that his natives would reject him. They did not have the arrogance to do that. They were good natives. They could fight in the bush, and try what they could. It was all futile. Being in Africa excited Charles, and he did not allow Nora's repeated warnings to tarnish what he felt for the veld, what his father before him had taught him to feel. But she would not stop her tarnishing of his dream.

"The papers say that most white people are leaving, because they believe we will lose the war."

Nora was accusing him of his failure to judge, to protect her. She goaded him with her remarks.

"Don't read the newspapers, Nora. You know how they exaggerate."

He regretted having brought the newspapers from the city, but she would have been upset if he had not brought them.

"We can go to Britain. Everyone is being allowed back. We could start all over again, Charles. I wish we could just pack our bags and leave."

"You never suggest moving to South Africa. You know I could be happy there. I cannot imagine myself waking up in England!"

When they stopped talking they did not touch. Instead, they moved away from each other. Nora went out, and admired the flowering bougainvillaea bush at the edge of the veranda, casting a purple glow over the marigolds below. The bees transferred pollen as they trespassed from one flower to the other, then buzzed away triumphantly. She was grateful for her escape, and her firm knowledge that he would not follow her. Did he think that she hated Africa? Did he not understand that it was only that she could not love it? She hated the unrest under the welcoming blue of the cloudless African sky.

Nora sat on her rocking chair at the edge of the veranda, behind the curtain of creeping ivy, and thought of the squatters, whom she distrusted. She was sure James's wife disliked her from the way she had behaved that time when she had gone to look for James, when they needed him to help push the truck. Two women had been sitting outside, almost identical in clothing made from the same cloth. She had stood at the edge of the clearing, and both women had ignored her, as though she was not even present. Why did they not stand up and abandon their task when they heard her dog bark? James's wife had picked up her basket and moved inside her hut, daring her to follow, knowing that she would have preferred to speak from outside the smoke-filled hut. Nora had followed, defiantly.

"I am looking for James. Is he home?" She had asked, aggressively.

"I haven't seen him, Madam."

Nora did not like the manner in which the woman said Madam, so much distaste wrapped around it. Nora stood in the dark hut, hating it, looking around at the objects thinly defined on the walls. There were dry maize cobs dangling from the roof, and soot that had turned the brown thatch of the hut to a deep black, and a set of small hoes hung from the mud walls. She hated it, and felt that she had trespassed. But this was her land, and these people were merely squatters, and she could send them away whenever it suited her. With this justification Nora stood her ground in the grass-thatched hut in which James's children had been born.

yes, but only in the hut

"Tell James to come and see me as soon as he comes home." She commanded. But she felt there were no secrets that she could keep from this woman, who looked at her without any fear.

"You can tell him yourself, Madam."

James had walked into the tension-filled room, then he walked away almost immediately with Madam, with the dog leading the way home.

James stood his ground, weighed down by the responsibility that he felt for his young brother, who needed land for his new family. What would he do without land on which to grow crops? He approached the veranda where he had observed Nora sitting, and noting that she was alone, took the chance to talk to her. He crouched humbly beneath the shed, till Nora turned to look at him. It was an uncomfortable moment when their eyes met, and they each knew that this time, whatever the cost, a decision would be made.

"I am asking for another piece of land, for my brother. He has taken a wife."

finally asking for land

19

As his words fell on her ears, she already knew their message, expected it. Her answer came fast upon her lips, defensively.

"Why do you ask me? Why do you not ask the Baas?"

She suggested many impossible actions, only to challenge him, so that he felt foolish. But he felt defiant still, and did not look at the ground when he spoke to her, which she read as a sign.

"Why can't you feed the family off the land that we have given you? We have already given you enough land to feed all your relatives."

He did not want to explain to her that the land was very little, that it was thorny and arid, and that nothing much grew there.

The bush war, which they were both aware of, made James's request sound like a challenge, a discarding of the restriction observed between those who serve and those whom they serve. She feared an unravelling of history which she could no longer dominate. His request, as she read it between his eyes, was like a claim.

She hated him for making her uncomfortable. If she told him that she would think about it, he would think she had made a firm promise. She must decide promptly what must be done, and he should not sense her hesitation, he must not read her anxiety which she felt overwhelm her. The settler had to maintain some superficial friendship with the squatters, to ensure their own safety.

In her paintings of Africa, Nora captured the flowers and trees and birds, but she was not able to paint the black faces. So she cast them in roles that she selected for them, and there was no need to see their faces. She saw them bent in labour on the farm, reaping the mealies, and they carried baskets of fruit on their heads. She saw them behind fires, and behind large calabashes of beer, and she painted them as dots scattered around a collection of huts. Nora never hung her pictures of Africa on the walls.

"I ask only to borrow your land, for use by my brother and his new wife. They would like to build a hut, and to grow a few crops."

Charles stepped on to the veranda, his blond hair waving over his sweaty forehead. He had heard the conversation through the door, and had waited to hear how Nora would handle it. His belief in her incompetence was confirmed by her long silences when the native spoke.

"James, don't bother Madam. I shall talk to you later. Go on."

Dismissed, James rose from his crouched position with a heavy heart. Why was it such a struggle for him to be granted a place to grow crops, a place which was not even being used. Charles turned his anger on Nora.

"Why do you let the natives get cheeky with you? Don't let them talk to you like that. You must not listen to their unreasonable demands."

Charles was not really angry at Nora on whom he spent his anger. He hated her patience, and felt she betrayed him to the natives.

"I had to hear him out, Charles. I told you he was here yesterday. How long shall we postpone the truth? We must prepare ourselves."

"There is no truth except the one that we allow. The natives cannot shape our history, or how we behave, or how we shall decide."

"What are we going to do about his request? What are we going to do? Are you going to give them the land?"

"I will give them the land. It still belongs to me, and I shall remind James of it. But this is the last time that I shall allow these kinds of demands. Don't allow them to talk to you like that, Nora. Do not allow them."

Charles was full of commands. His mind wove imaginary spaces in the air and he did not hear the roaring river engulf the bank. He could not emerge out of the mist and allow history to degrade him. His eyes were brimming with hostile tears as he looked down at her, and she feared him. The dark smoke from the edge of the farm hastened to the sky, and she feared that even more.

The news of the downed aeroplane came in the morning over the wireless. It was reported that all the passengers had been killed.

The news came to the squatters, who had no radio, through a passerby several days later. The old man received the news from where he sat in the shed, and shook his head vigorously, as though the flies bothered him. This piece of news confirmed that the Africans indeed commanded guns that could reach into the sky, and bring down the white man's machine. It surprised him that this was possible, but he did not know that he should rejoice. What would the white men do after being challenged in this manner? Would they not revenge the death of so many of their kind? It terrified the old man to think deeply on it, or consider the actions anger might unleash. These were indeed hard times, and the old man wondered if he had enough time to see the crisis to its end. The voices of the children as they played came faintly to him through the shade. They were playing a game in which they counted stones into a hole.

Behind where the children sat the maize had grown tall and shiny, waving golden heads at the sky, their tassels a sign that the cobs would soon mature. The stalks had grown sturdy, in readiness to support the cobs, which would be heavy when they had ripened. The vaulting leaves were broader and longer. There was nothing much to do in the fields but wait. The family spent the time around their own huts, tending their small gardens, except James, who still had to work in the main house.

MaMoyo, whom they also called Mavis, did not like her life on the farm. The knowledge that several generations of her husband's family had laboured fruitlessly on this farm intensified her dissatisfaction. She told herself that her main concern was for her daughter, whom she feared would also have to work on the farm as she had done. She wanted a different future for her daughter. Perhaps an education would release her from this continued design, which was almost becoming its own tradition, though everyone loathed a life in which they owned nothing.

The city–her daughter would find employment in the city, which beckoned with a different kind of freedom. James would not listen to her argument. Mavis had gone to the city once, before she got married, to visit an aunt. Her aunt lived in a small house at the edge of the city. People in the city were not well off, certainly, but they appeared to her freer. Her family were not wanted on this farm, though they provided ample labour. It was felt that the migrant labourers were easier to control, because they were desperate for work, and were strangers on this land.

The old man hated the life on the farm, and he wished that he could make the journey back to his home, from where he had been uprooted as a boy.

"You are too old for such a journey," they told him. "You would not survive such a journey."

But he insisted, and so they stopped listening to him. Why had he not gone back when he was younger, and his feet had the strength to carry him? Why must he bother them with his unattainable desires? The old man mourned as he sat under the shed behind the hut. He had worked on this land too, but he had never felt at home on it.

The mealie-porridge boiled on the hearth, and the children played outside, racing around the yard in circles. MaMoyo felt her wish coming upon her again–to take them to a school in the town. There were better teachers there, and her children would learn more. The teachers in the bush schools had hardly passed for their certificates.

"There you are. I had begun to wonder when you might come home."

She looked up from the fire she had been tending, feeling uncomfortable because of what had been going through her mind.

"It is not as late as all that. Is there something that you would like me to do for you?"

She went back to tending the fire, which she poked with a wide stick.

"I thought we might talk a little. Did you hear about the plane being shot down?"

Now she looked up, and he understood that she had a lot more on her mind. It would be impolite to continue the conversation while he stood in the doorway like a stranger. He covered the distance between them by pulling up a stool and drawing close to where she sat near the fire, her legs folded beneath her. There was a long interval before he gave his answer, while he prepared his place to sit, and that gave the impression that he was considering her question more thoroughly.

"Moses told me about it. A lot of people were killed, all those in the plane. Their bodies were burnt. I wonder what will happen now. They say the people are very angry, in the city."

He regarded her carefully as he spoke, but she did not look at him, only at the fire which sparked a blue flame between them. When her answer came, it was delivered in slow and careful tones. She did not want to anger him.

"But that is how a fight is waged. Worse things are likely to happen. Don't you think?"

He was surprised by her willingness to dismiss the fatality as something that did not affect them. But he agreed with her, because it was true that worse things were to be expected.

"I suppose we should expect more bloodshed. I am glad we are not in the city where most of the anger is. I wonder how it must be, to be in the city on such a day as this."

It was clear he did not want to be in the city. It was not a matter of the plane, but rather that he preferred it here. She did not share his stagnancy, and felt that she should express her resentment of his immobility. Why could they not move from this farm?

"I still think our children would be better off if we moved to the city. Their future would be more assured. Why must they grow up only to work on this farm? Who knows how long it will be before this Independence that we wish for the country will come? We might both be old, like your father there under the shed, and our children will be looking after us, right on this farm."

She dropped the stick with which she stirred the fire, and gathering her clothes around her she stood up, and walked to the wall where she pulled a pot from a nail. She could not sit still while she felt his resentment and his resistance. It was a small hut, and there was not much space for her to move around, away from him.

"Things will change soon. I am sure of it. There is no need for us to leave."

She knew he would not budge from his resolution, and she wished she had not even started the discussion. She sat down again, to be polite to him, even though she wanted to move into the air outside.

"I believe we should leave, to protect our children. It will not be easy there for us. But think of the children. Think of how much they will gain by our action. We can both find jobs there to support the children."

She knew that she only spoke to the wind, because he would not listen.

"The jobs will not be different from the ones we have here except that we would no longer have our family around us. Must we take the children away from their family?"

He did not see that even now they did not have their family, that each of them nurtured a resentment that left them incomplete. They had nothing to give to each other, nothing that was completely their own.

"We can come back to visit, and even bring gifts for the family."

He answered her rapidly, as though she had lost her mind. He was impatient with her, though he would rather not be, because she resented it.

"What use are gifts to our family? Will that restore their dignity? Do you know how cruel life in the city can be? Some people have no jobs, they sleep in the streets. Not all the children there grow up to be teachers. How about your aunt? How does she pay her rent when she does not have a job? Is that the life you want for your children?"

"My aunt had no education when she went to the city. My children will go to school, surely that should stop them from that kind of life?"

"But you cannot be sure, can you? At least here I can be sure that my children can grow up with a sense of decency, respecting their elders. We should wait and see what the changes that will come will be like, for I am sure what has happened now will have some effect."

She was burdened by the need to see her children advance, and paid no attention to the hope he held out, which she could not believe. It was easier for her to think of action, than of waiting, doing nothing. Had they not done enough of waiting? If she could move she would have achieved something. If she could pick up her problems and carry them to new ground, that would satisfy her. Why must he dangle this hope to her, and use it against her? Whenever she thought of the old man, she saw the folly of not acting on one's hope. The old man had not gone to his village, though it would have made him happy merely to see the place. Even if he had gone five years ago, he might have arrived there. Now he ceaselessly pronounced the name of that distant place, which none of them had seen.

"You want us to wait, then?"

She spoke softly, almost to herself, and he did not answer her. Since it was clear that they had finished talking, or that he no longer wished to talk, she went outside, and walked a little. He valued the past over the present, and saw it replicated in the future. James's history felt burdensome to her, and it hurt her, and her children. He was not an active man, and she pitied him. Time would not move towards them, they had to move towards it, if it was to find them whole. The present, as they lived it, would not be satisfied by waiting. He was immobile, like his father whom they had to carry from shed to hut and from hut to shed, every day. He took pleasure in his hope for redress, which he saw approaching in the future. Meanwhile, their lives must be dry, and they must live in the ruins of that past which they carried always with them. Why must they be trapped in the memory of an old man who could not walk? For the woman, the shattering indignity of her poverty had destroyed the prestige of the past. She was afraid that they would not recognize themselves in the future, either as they thought they were, or as they would like to be.

Independence Day

"Move back! Move back!" the policemen shouted.

Today they were lining the main street in the city to see the Prince who had come from England to give their country back to them. At midnight.

The woman took shelter in the green space in her head, and waited. The children, released early from school, were standing along a stretch of empty road, books held above their heads casting inky shadows on their faces. The sun shone brightly on the tarred road. A policeman stood on the broad yellow centre line, his starched cap exploring the distance. Policemen in heavy brown boots and khaki uniforms, holding guns and batons, told the children to move back. The Prince from England would not like to be crowded upon.

On the other side of the road women were dancing and singing traditional songs, under the towering gum tree. Sweat poured down their faces as they welcomed the future. The policemen with guns and batons told them to move to the back of the crowd or line up with the rest of the people. One gave them tiny flags to wave, a new flag for a new nation. While waiting for the Prince, sent by his mother the Queen, the woman held a branch from a jacaranda bush over her tired face, and stayed shielded in the green space in her head.

A limousine came down the street that was lined with exploding purple jacarandas. Children broke into screams, thinking it was the very important person who had come all the way from England to give them back their country. The woman watched the car drive up, and then heard the excitement die down. This was not the moment. It was just another car.

"We shall not know which car the Prince is in when he finally drives by," a man said. "For security reasons. But we have to wave at all the cars as they drive by. One of them has the Prince."

"You mean we shall not see the Prince?" the woman asked, perplexed. She had woken up very early, to see the man who had the power to give them back their country. She heard the sound of sirens, and saw policemen rush by on motorbikes, followed by several cars moving slowly behind.

"Stay back! Stay back!" the policemen shouted to the excited students who extended their arms and waved their tiny flags in front of the stream of passing vehicles.

"Which car has the Prince?" asked the woman.

"Certainly not the first or the second one, for security reasons," the man answered. "And certainly not the last, it's too obvious."

It must be the third then. The woman looked hard through the heavily tinted windows, but saw nothing. Still, everyone waved and shouted. They saw only their own excited faces, intercepted among reflections of purple jacaranda blooms. Along that very road the Prince surely had passed. If they had not seen him, maybe he had seen them. "Did you see the Prince?" they asked each other on the way home. Later, some of them would see him at the stadium, at midnight. The woman would not go.

The man kept one arm around the woman, while with the other he held a bottle of cold beer. He had the television on, and insisted that he would watch the Independence celebrations first. He had already given her the money, and she kept it knotted in a yellow handkerchief which she had tied on the strap of her bra. The stadium, usually reserved for soccer matches, was filled to capacity. First there was traditional dancing in the middle of the stadium. The woman withdrew into the safe space in her mind, and watched the pictures go by on the screen.

The new Prime Minister gave a long speech, and people clapped and shouted. They raised their fists in jubilation. The new Prime Minister spoke into a microphone. The women continued dancing while the Prime Minister was speaking. The people waved their flags when they were told everything would be changing soon. Jobs and more money. Land and education. Wealth and food. The woman saw the Prince sitting quietly, dressed in spotless white clothing. They said his mother could not come. But in these matters he was as important as his mother. The new Prime Minister said something about the Prince, and everyone cheered.

The man watching the screen went to the kitchen for another beer. He was going to celebrate Independence properly: with cold beer and a woman. Now it was ten minutes to midnight. She must take her clothes off. The screen flashed the ticking minutes. The Prince and the new Prime Minister walked to the large flagpole in the middle of the stadium. The old flag was flapping in the air, the new one was hanging below. The man pushed the woman onto the floor. He was going into the new era in style and triumph. She opened her legs. It was midnight, and the new flag went up. The magic time of change. Green, yellow, white. Food, wealth, reconciliation.

When he was through he sent her home. When he awoke he preferred the whole house to himself. They had met under the jacarandas, waiting for the English Prince.

In the morning she saw miniature flags caught along the hedge: the old flag and the new.

The Shoemaker

"Knock harder! He is in there!"

"What makes you think so? He is not answering. The door is locked." The girl pulled forcefully at the handle, but it resisted. She held her face contorted against the burning sun, through which they had walked. Bright metallic bangles jingled along her right arm, as she let go of the handle. Her ears were pierced with wide gashes through which large triangular earrings hung, and dangled along her bare neck.

"I know he is in there. I can smell the cooking. He has been eating." The second girl moved to the side of the shop and tried to see through the window but the glass was opaque with dirt. She rubbed vigorously at it with a handkerchief that she held balled in her hand, wetting it repeatedly with her saliva. Her efforts to clear the pane were futile, and she withdrew from her task. The shoemaker had not inconvenienced himself with a curtain. When his privacy mattered, he put an old newspaper against the pane. And that was only when he went away for a few days, to visit his relatives in the country. To do that he lay on the small creaky bed in the dark, and travelled through his mind. He always arrived. He boasted to the women of his ability to travel in this way. It was easier than digging up graves, he said. His relatives had died in the war.

The door opened suddenly and the two girls stepped back in surprise, though they had been insisting that the shoemaker was indeed inside. Most of the shoemaker's customers were women.

"We nearly left. Why do you lock yourself in, in midday light? We nearly left." The girl shrugged her rounded shoulders, to show her dissatisfaction. She was tall, and her hair was plaited with thick black thread, then lined on the sides of her head, so that one could see her skin where the hair had been pulled away. Her eyes, sparkling with gaiety, moved with familiarity over the shoemaker. She ridiculed him a little, through the way her eyes travelled over him, searchingly. She wore a red dress, spotted generously with sad black dots.

"But you didn't, did you?" the shoemaker chuckled, wiping his eyes vigorously to adjust to the light. He moved a small wooden stool which was along the walls, and drew it into the shed. The inside of his shop was very dark. The only source of light was the doorway. The light cut diametrically into the room, without seeming to illuminate any particular object. The shop had a low roof which made it necessary to bend very low to get in. Inside there was nowhere for a visitor to sit. The third person had to crouch outside the doorway. Most of the room was taken up by shoes. Women's shoes. One wondered if anyone had ever come back to collect their shoes after leaving them here.

The second girl watched the shoemaker with interest, finding him curious and appealing in his eccentric life in the shed. She wore a black dress, though the sun was hot, and it absorbed the heat. It was an old dress, frayed along the hem, but she seemed hardly conscious of its age. Her face was rather intense, and she did not say much after her frantic knocking on the door.

"I like red shoes. I always sew them first," the shoemaker said as he received the shoes from the two women, and then looked around for his snuff box. There were several red shoes on his tiny bed. The walls of the shop were made of sheets of zinc. At noon the sheets were very hot. When it cooled, towards evening, you heard them crackling. The shoemaker talked to himself while he worked. He sat in the stream of light at the doorway, and plunged the rest of the room into darkness.

"Why don't you sit outside? You are always at the doorway. You should sit outside where it is cooler," the woman in red dress suggested.

"I prefer to be inside. Don't you?" The shoemaker stared at the girl, questioningly. He was not talking about his shop.

"Inside your shop?" the girl asked with suspicion, and laughed.

"Inside my shop," the shoemaker said, and he left the girls for his travels. The war, however, made it difficult to think of the village before its devastation. Once in a while, the shoemaker caught a glimpse of his mother carrying water from the stream, while he sat carving at the back of the hut with his grandfather. A small branch kept the water on his mother's head from lapping about. It always amazed him how she balanced her load freely, without supporting it with her arms.

"We like it better out here, in the bright sun," the girl persisted. She spoke for herself, but drew in her partner who remained silent, so that her statement sounded more forceful. Why did her friend not say something, to support her, against this man who appeared to her absurd?

"But this is not your shop," he said, mockingly. The two girls looked at each other. Then they both looked at the shoemaker who was threading his needle, surprised that he would invest such pride in a shoddy place like this. His head leaned further out of the shop as he tried to gather enough light, to assist him in his task.

The two women got tired of standing, and began leaning on one another. The girl in the red dress had her elbow resting on the taller girl, and they both continued looking with curiosity at the man. It was late afternoon, and they did not have much to do till evening, when they would rush home and prepare something to eat. The tall girl furrowed her brow. She did not like the sun getting into her eyes. The shoemaker whistled a tune. He had finally managed to thread the needle.

"Why are you not married?" the tall girl asked. "Are you afraid of women?" He did not answer immediately, but went on with his task. He did not even appear to have heard the question. Maybe he had heard it many times.

"It is easy to marry a woman. It takes courage to be alone. It takes courage to be alive. Sometimes." He still did not look up from his work. The silent girl sought the man's face, pursuing the thing which had put the sadness in his voice, for it was unmistakable. But still she did not say anything, or feel the need to speak.

"It is not easy to marry a woman," the tall girl insisted. "First you have to find a woman who wants to marry you." She threw her hands slightingly at the shoemaker, taunting him.

"And you think that is hard in this township?" the shoemaker asked. He looked up briefly from his sewing. He searched his surroundings, and appeared assured that any woman would find them adequate.

"I wouldn't want to live with all these shoes, and customers knocking on the door all day," the tall girl said, as though in possession of some secret that the man could never guess at. She laughed nervously.

"I haven't asked you to marry me," the shoemaker said gently.

He held the red shoe lovingly. It seemed to give him pain to force the needle through its leather. He bit his lower lip as he pushed at the thick needle. It was hot inside the shed, and sweat ran down the side of his ears. He wiped it off with his shoulder, raising his arm a little and bending his head.

"Why don't you live somewhere, in a house? With relatives or friends. Why do you live in your shop?" the tall girl asked.

"My relatives are buried. I like it in my shop." He stood up, and disappeared into the darkness of the shop. He scrambled for something under his bed, and when he had found it, returned to his stool at the doorway and sat down again. His face was held tightly, as though something threatened to break in him. He held back the pain of an old memory, which he held between his shaking hands. The tall girl, her bright eyes suddenly vacant, was thinking of the men who were leaving for the bush. So many men. Her brother had left, without even saying goodbye to their mother, or to her. She wondered if she should leave too. To go home and prepare the evening meal. The shoemaker was holding an old yellow newspaper which showed his village after it had been raided and burnt down by the security forces. Members of his village had been accused of participating with freedom fighters. He had escaped, narrowly.

"There is nothing to go back to," the tall girl said. "Nothing. And you are a good shoemaker." She looked away at the woman carrying a baby on her back, walking on the other side of the street. Why was the baby crying so much?

"All burned, burned, burned," the shoemaker said, as though to banish the image that forced itself into his mind. He threw the paper onto the bed and picked up the red shoe. It was easier to deal with an old shoe than with an old memory.

The tall girl was tired of her friend's weight on her shoulder, and shrugged her off. Perhaps her friend's silence made her lose her equilibrium, in the matter that she provoked between her and the shoemaker. Why did she not say something? It was unlike her to be so silent. Should they not go home? she asked.

"I am not ready to go home yet," the girl answered, breaking her silence, and found a spot on the ground where she sat with her back to the shoemaker. She held the folds of her black dress between her legs, her face expressionless.

Shelling Peanuts

"Take cover! Take cover!"

The small boys run through the streets and the yards carrying AK-rifles. They shoot through the hedges and yell as they drop to the ground, then rise again to confront each other. They contort their faces, making them as diabolical as possible. They want to look mean and merciless. They imitate the rut-a-tut sound of bursting fire. The girls watch and laugh gleefully as the boys roll themselves on the ground and hide behind tall grasses and imaginary protective rocks.

"You are cheating. I said 'Take cover!' but you kept on running. You don't know how to play this game. If I say 'Take cover!' you must lie down and hide. It means I am going to shoot at the enemy or else the enemy is going to shoot."

"We should start again. We need more people to make the game exciting. Let us call the girls to join us, then we can have two teams."

"Girls don't know how to fight and they cry if you push them. I don't think we should call the girls into our team."

"Not all girls cry if you push them. Rebecca doesn't cry. Let's call her, then there will be four of us."

"My mother told me that some women have also gone to fight and that they hold big guns and fight beside the men. I have seen pictures of dead women who have been killed by the soldiers in *The African Times*. My uncle shows them to us. This means we must call the girls to join us."

"Okay then. But let us decide first how we are going to play the game. You two are going to be the soldiers and I will be the rebel with Rebecca. You must first of all tell us your demands, then we will refuse. You must then go away and we will start fighting. If we shoot and you haven't said 'Take cover' then you are captured. We must also wear the banana leaves as helmets and paint our faces. What are your demands?"

"We want more money. We want to know why you cannot make enough money in your machine to give to everyone?"

The mother watched from where she sat under a shade, listening to the boys argue and decide. Her cheeks shivered slightly, though her eyes were dry of tears. She held her knitting needles tightly together between her outstretched legs. A basket of unshelled peanuts rested on one side of the mat. She watched her daughter Rebecca join the boys in the fight for territory, and was disturbed. Was it possible the daughter and the father were at this moment carrying out the same act? They had never met. The father and the daughter.

"Take cover! Take cover!" the daughter shouted. The woman was in an agony of recollection. She put the needles aside, picked up the basket of peanuts, and folded her legs under her. The shade had shifted a little and she got up to move her mat to the other side of the tree.

"You're dead! You're dead!" the children's voices pierced the air. They dived into the hedge, raising small clouds of dust behind them, their bare feet protruding beneath the shadows.

The woman thought about the face that she remembered, scanning in her mind the broad shoulders, the muscular arms, and she was afraid. A young man not much older than herself, then. What would she do now that she was carrying his child? He said he couldn't stay, as he had already made plans to leave. He had not thought that their circumstances would change, that a baby would be on the way.

"I shot you! You're dead . . . stop cheating!" Rebecca shouted indignantly. The young boy only laughed, then turned rapidly around in mock anger, his brow contorted, firing a chain of bullets towards her. The mother heard the shrieking voice of her daughter, then the pleading tones of the father whose memory was awakened.

"We shall start all over when I return," he had told her.

"When you return?" she echoed. "Will you return?" He looked away to his trousers which were torn at the knees.

"Those who have no jobs have to leave. There is a job out there." In his mind he meant no place in particular, only a piece of battleground in the bush, where he could claim some territory.

"What shall I do," she asked seeking his eyes, "on my own?"

He did not answer. Perhaps he was ashamed of what he could not do for her.

"Take cover! Take cover!" the children's guns sent metallic fire over the roof tops.

"We shall wipe you out!" the daughter shouted.

The mother, disturbed, could not bear her daughter's determined voice. She wanted to call her and send her to the shops, or give her some woman's duty in the house. She saw the daughter's legs disappearing behind the tree under which she sought shade, and saw a small boy run after her, clutching a hand grenade.

"Surrender," the little boy said as the two struggled behind the tree. The mother closed her eyes in search of the missing face.

The man, standing up, was about to leave but kept looking at the woman, whom he was seeing for the last time. Perhaps she would say or do something to make him stay. Not only today, but for good. But what could she say? Everything had come to her already decided. She could not reshape what had come to her complete, already out of reach. Only something of the man was left with her, and she had to nurture it, inside her. The man stared again at the woman, wanting to touch her for the last time, but he wanted her to come forward, to give herself. She would not do it, however, and he left.

The dead ones got up and walked. In the noonday heat the children ran around in circles, tiring of their game. They were laughing at each other and at the silliness of their sport. The mother had shelled the peanuts into a small basket which she secured steadily with her knees. Each of the children withdrew into his own world, lying under the shade of the green hedge and recovering his energy.

"You're dead! You're dead!" The children mocked the collapse of their fantastic visions, as the game drew to an end and the mother welcomed the quiet that followed their play.

The mother knew that if they invented another game, they would all jump up in enthusiasm, if it pleased them to do so. She called Rebecca, and sent her inside the house with the shelled peanuts.

It Is Hard to Live Alone

It was not always possible to get fresh vegetables at the market, but Rudo liked to go there anyway to chat with the other women. Each seller had a small stall on which were arranged onions, tomatoes, cabbages, and potatoes. The tomatoes would be arranged in neat pyramids that would gain the attention of prospective customers. The women huddled in corners where they would chat and laugh loudly, keeping an eye on their stalls, and jumping up if a customer chanced to come by.

Sometimes the vendor would approach only when you began to move away, hoping that her activity would oblige you to buy from her. If you decided to go ahead and buy from the next stall, the woman you had left behind would stand and watch the whole process. You could feel her eyes and you would become really nervous and wish she would actually say something horrid. The woman at the new stall might run out of newspapers to wrap your tomatoes in, and she would have to go to the other woman who was staring at you. So you would wait even longer and wonder why buying a few tomatoes should get as complicated as all that.

It pleased Rudo to see that the women had a big fire roaring at the edge of their stalls, because it was a cold day. There was MaDube coming in with a big dish of dried fish balanced on her head, her arms hanging at her sides. She was a large, powerful woman who was also not afraid to state her opinion. People whispered that she was involved with the recruitment of freedom fighters. As a woman, she would be less suspicious to the authorities. But it was rumoured that women were actually being trained to fight in the bush alongside the men. It was amazing to hear such reports. MaDube was laughing boisterously, telling the other women about how she had managed to get her money from a man who had taken some fish from her on credit and had been avoiding her since. MaDube's arms were balanced assertively along her waist as she told the tale, dramatically. Everyone in the group laughed. "Well, let me put my fish on display along my counter. MaMoyo, did you sell anything today?" she asked, preoccupied with her activity.

MaMoyo, recovering from her laughter answered after a long pause in which she took in a large gasp of air, "Not a thing. In fact, if I don't manage to sell something today my son will not be able to attend school tomorrow. His school fees are due." MaMoyo's laughter had subsided, and when she bent down and threw a log onto the fire, it crackled and burst into flame.

MaMlambo spoke, her voice sad and mirthless. "It is such a cold day. I wish I didn't have to spend the day waiting. I wish something would happen, anything. I am tired of waiting. Where are the customers? Sometimes I wonder if I am ever going to make enough." Her words were addressed to no one in particular, and they drifted away unacknowledged.

MaMpofu beat her skirts determinedly, as though ridding them of dust or smoky air, then she said, "They say that things will change one day. That we shall all have more to eat and that education will soon be free." Now her arms rested motionless on her crossed knees. Her eyes were pinned on MaSibanda, who said the first thing that came to her mind.

"It is hard for me to live without a man in the home, but we all need to be strong." She reached out with her hands and extended her palms to the leaping flames. Instantly, she withdrew them and moved cautiously away from the flame, uncertain how much distance she should maintain between herself and the fire.

Rudo's attention moved from one woman to the other, and she

caught what they said with interest. She did not feel the need to interrupt them with her purchase.

"Do you know, that woman MaNdlovu, who always comes here is barren," MaMlambo said. "She can not bear any children for her husband. It is a terrible thing to be barren. The worst thing is, if you never have a child with your husband when you die they throw a rat into your grave, just to show how useless you were. How can you claim to be a woman without knowing the joy and pain of childbirth? A woman who has never suckled a child on her breast is not a complete woman."

"Barren! That is a terrible thing. She must be ashamed of herself. If I was barren I would not know how to live. I would not be able to hold my head up in front of other women." MaMpofu shook her head fiercely to emphasize the point and beat her palms together in bewilderment. This was not enough to jar MaSibanda into the discussion.

"I don't have a man. It is hard to live alone. I wish I had a man in the house. It is so tough to be a woman and to be on your own." The flames were dying down. MaSibanda moved briefly towards the burning embers, then withdrew, realizing that the fire was hotter than she had imagined. The heat kept on changing and she kept on readjusting her position. She decided to move in as near to the fire as possible, then covered her legs with the material of her dress which she gathered from her sides and piled to the front.

MaMpofu, moving around MaDube's counter and rearranging the tomatoes added, "I have six children and another on the way. If there is one thing I'm not it is barren ... and yet, once I tell a man that I am expecting his child, I never see him again."

"I have four children, but my husband has impregnated my younger sister who has been living with us. We only have one room that we live in and there is no privacy. I think that is why my husband got tempted. They say a man is like a dog, you can't leave a strip of meat lying around and expect that he will not eat it." MaMlambo's face was contorted in disgust, she looked as though she was about to spit to the ground. Rudo moved to the other side of the stall and sat next to MaDube who had started knitting.

MaSibanda held a long stick in her hand and poked at the fire absent-mindedly. She threw some orange peels from the pocket of her dress into the fire. She watched them slowly twist and hiss and start to burn. She shifted her body away from the direction of the acrid smoke.

She approached the fire from the other side and drew closer than she had been before, compensating for the cold wind that she felt on her back. "How I wish I had a man at home. It is hard to live alone. It is hard to be a woman living alone without a man." The discussion went on without her.

MaMpofu would not let the blame lie entirely on the man. "I think your young sister knew exactly what she was doing. If I were you I would kick her right out of my home. My six children each have a different father but it is not my fault you know, each father just left before they were born. But I have done my job as a woman."

MaDube, who had been silent for a time, interjected. "These are difficult times to bring a child into the world. Every woman who is raising a son is raising a soldier. It is hard for a woman to raise a child that might have to go back into the soil. It is hard for women to bear sons for men that are leaving, men that might not be there to see them grow. Ask MaMoyo here whose husband had to leave. Rudo, what would you like to buy and cook for that young man of yours?"

"The dried fish will do. I will have a few tomatoes as well. It is a cold day, it is good that you have the fire going." The discussion of the older women had made Rudo thoughtful.

"Sit down and chat with us a while. Tell us about that young man of yours. You young people are so secretive. Are you planning to have any children yet? If you are having problems with that, you need some medicine to get cleansed so that you can conceive."

"Or maybe she needs something, to help things along, you know." MaMoyo, listening from the other side of the stall, shouted an opinion. Everyone laughed knowingly, and Rudo felt embarrassed.

"It is not that at all. I would like to have a child but I feel really afraid. There are so many women with no husbands but with a lot of children. I do not want to be one of them. The country is in a state of confusion. Who knows what the rules are any more? Who knows what to do? Who knows what is really important? We only know our loss and our fear and our silence. We know we are women asked to bear children. We know that to bear children will bring us suffering. This land must be watered with the blood of our children and with the saltiness of our tears before we can call it our own. What shall I tell my child about the father who is absent?"

"You speak like a grownup," MaDube responded. "There is no time for childhood fears or hopes or dreams. Women are the backbone of this struggle. If people like you are barren because they are afraid what shall be the result of that? Let life flow through you, my child. We need sons to take the places of those whose bodies lie without proper burial. Our sons shall be the ones to continue with the struggle, for who knows how long it will be. The earth is very angry. The land needs to be purified, it is too much burdened with the blood of young people. It was never the case when our ancestors lived that the death of young men came before that of old incapacitated men. We must purify the blood flowing on the land with fresh milk springing from our breasts. We must fill the land with the innocence and joy of young ones. It is our task as women and as mothers."

"You do speak well, MaDube, but your words do not give me comfort. What about our daughters. Will they find husbands to marry them?"

"The day might be nearer than you think. Take these onions and go home to prepare for your husband. It is a cold day and a man likes to find a warm meal after work."

MaSibanda held the stick in a tight grip in her hand, stirring the grey powder that covered the embers. She threw the stick away and held her arms across her cold breasts. The air around her ears shivered.

"I do wish I had a man at home. It is so hard to live alone. A man would make all the difference in my life."

"I have always been afraid to find out where all my men have gone to," MaMpofu said. "I just sit by my door and wait. Imagine if at the end of the war six husbands come back to me!"

Moon on the Water

The sounds alternated throughout the night: loud, raspy snoring, and
urine cascading into a chamber pot.

The chamber pot was not the manufacturer's porcelain model: it
was a masterpiece of domestic handiwork. You could assess the rise
and fall of the family's fortunes just by looking at. If it wore a new,
shiny aspect, the family had just emptied a three-litre can of cooking
oil. From the bold label, Olivine or Roil, you could tell how generous
the purchase had been. When the oil was getting low in the can, it was
hard not to think of a similarly viscous and tinted liquid with a more
penetrating smell. These cans were not strong and rusted easily.
Grandpa sliced the top off, working at it steadily with a small knife.
When he was through, the top edges of the tin looked alarmingly
sharp.

The pot took pride of place at the head of the bed. On days when
Grandpa forgot to empty the tin, Grandma would ask one of us to do
it. It was hard to keep the pot from your face, since there was no handle, and one had to embrace the offending liquid which lapped
threateningly against the sides. Grandpa produced an amazing
amount of urine. Sometimes he would empty the container several

times during the night, passing over our heads with the pungent pot held between his palms like an ancestral gourd.

Inside the house, my eyes are drawn to the goatskin. It is laid beside the bed. In his youth Grandpa had suffered from tuberculosis and recovered. But he had retained a habit of spitting. Throughout the night he had the spitting urges. He would roll, lean over and spit, then roll back to sleep. The goatskin alternated between states of wetness and dryness, its hairs gradually falling out in patches. When it was hairless, Grandpa would look for a new goatskin. The goatskin before me had hairs that were twisted in dry phlegm, and others that lay together in a thin mass. Grandma would get up one morning, grab a stick from outside, then push the goatskin outside where it would dry in the scorching sun. When you walked into her room for the first time, she would say, "Keep off Grandpa's goatskin." Once she was sick, and when the women from the church came to see her, she kept waving her arms about, her chest was too sore for her to speak. They all left thinking that she had seen the holy ghost–but Grandma always hated to see anyone step on that goatskin.

When we arrived at new places to which we had travelled to visit relations, Grandpa would gather the soil of the land, letting it rest on his palm. Squatting froglike in the characteristic pose of ancestral address, he would mix the soil and the water. Of these muddy waters he would have us drink. It was an initiation and a rite that united us with our new spaces and released the spirit. Locked in childhood innocence, we felt safe, we felt happy, as the soft scent of decaying vegetation tickled our nostrils.

News has just reached us that Grandfather has died. He had spurned the alien atmosphere of the white-washed walls and the attention of those white-coated young people, poking their instruments at him. Where was the dignity in death if one was not in one's home? His death had been unheralded by the restless mooing of the head bull in the kraal of his village. Instead, his breath had left him in mid-day light, without ceremony.

I am trying, laboriously, to remember Grandfather. It is not that I have forgotten him, but something in my mind fights the recall of his image. My intense concentration leads me, absurdly, to his toes. They seemed to flare out in defiance and protest at the idea of being confined in a pair of shoes. I had often thought of purchasing shoes for him, but the memory of those disapproving toes had banished the intent. A dark spot on the nail of the big toe had inspired Grandfather to make up several tales, each more improbable than the last. A tale of night magic would begin with some reference to the dark spot: it was the mark of a great tribe that had long since vanished, sometimes it was the mark of a witches' curse, it meant Grandfather had been a leopard once. It was also the curse of a maiden whom he had left for Grandmother.

I hear the sound of the train as it goes by. It sounds unfamiliar, breaking my efforts at remembering, and I walk outside and stand in the orchard. The street lights come on, casting a yellow luminescence over the dark macadam road. Insects rise along the road and grow into an ever-increasing ball of flying creatures which hit against the elongated fluorescent lamp. The light casts uncertain rays on the wide mango leaves, turning them to a dusky colouring that reminds me of death. The inside of my mouth feels dry, as though I have swallowed a handful of dust. A dog barks in the distance and a set of startled birds flies off in unison from below the tree where large rotten mangoes pattern the ground.

Grandfather could not justify parting with twenty cents to buy a new toothbrush. He would use a brush till all its bristles had fallen out. It was painful to watch him applying vigorous strokes with the bare plastic handle, his zeal undaunted. In a single day he could put his signature on a new brush: its bristles were parted in the middle and pointed in entirely different directions.

A week ago, my grandfather sat with me under the veranda eating mangoes: yellow juice ran down coarse, grooved fingers, taking a path along the furrows of wrinkled flesh on his hands, and I watched it disappear inside the brown jacket. Now I walk to the veranda in search of that elusive moment.

"I wish I had stayed in the village. This life in the city has been difficult for me. When your father died and your mother disappeared into the city, your grandmother wondered if we would be able to bring up four grandchildren. But we managed, and here you are. If anything happens to me I would like to go back. That is my only solace." I responded disinterestedly, telling my brother Tafadzwa casually to turn off the radio. The cement floor of the veranda bears no memory of that day when the large drops of juice had formed extensive sticky marks on the floor.

Sad rays of yellow light from the street lamps form straight, narrow beams that sparkle and glitter as they hit the tiny pools of water still held in the grooves along the imperfect road.

Grandfather walked barefoot, his flapping khaki trousers torn along the edges. He had been sick once and we had taken him to the hospital. He had insisted on walking to the ambulance waiting at the gate, rather than being carried on a stretcher brought by the men in white coats.

We discussed it and decided that if he went back to live in the country, the medications he needed for his illness would not be available. The armed struggle had destroyed his village, there was no solace there.

I have been outside longer than I realize. The sky fills with a myriad sparkling stars. The white, dazzling moon is reflected in a bucket of water. I dip my hand into it, and see the reflection ripple and disappear and the moon's light break into shimmering wet pieces. As the water settles, I see the moon form its image again. I stir the water gently, and once again its light sparkles and loses shape. As I let the water settle once more, the moon's image fails to gather itself. Up in the sky, I see that the moon has hidden itself under a cloud.

A Thunderstorm

The kitchen smelled of fish. When Tsitsi dropped the onions into the pan, the oil sizzled. She retreated from the sputtering liquid, bumping into Dube, her father-in-law, as he made his entrance.

"Careful now, my child. The food smells really good."

"Oh, it's only a bit of fish I got from the market." Tsitsi was not able to say much today. She had spent the day thinking about having a child and her earlier convictions had been eroded. Her inability to decide altogether if she should have a child yet frustrated her.

The bright yellow paint they had used for the kitchen walls gave the room an unnatural yellow glow. Ponderayi, her husband, had bought the thick fluorescent paint from the road workers who had come to place markings on the road. The bargain had been hard to resist, but the paint was already beginning to peel.

"Do you think we should have used that paint from the road to cover the walls?" Tsitsi asked. "It looks bad now. Our walls flash at people as they pass down the street." Tsitsi felt confused. It was not fair to make this trivial judgement when she had not protested earlier as the paint was applied. Dube looked at the paint, without emotion. The bulb dimmed and went off, plunging the room into darkness.

Tsitsi opened the window and drew the curtain, letting in the light from the street lamps. It flooded through in a slanted path into the middle of the room.

"I will find a candle," Dube said as he went out of the kitchen into the bedroom. She heard him curse as he bumped into an obstacle in the dark. In a little while he returned, his path lit by a short flickering blue-and-red flame from a small candle. The candle, not being generous in its light, fought the darkness with dim flashes. Yellow patches leapt sporadically from the wall as the light alternately grew and diminished. It seemed to leap and lick the wall then rest briefly to repeat the action once more.

A gust of wind surprised them. It blew the curtain which hung along a wire which was held on to the wall by a pair of nails. The curtain released its loose grip on the wall and came down onto the cement floor. Sand trickled down from the nail holes. Although Tsitsi had always known that the curtain needed fixing, the incident surprised her. She stood staring at the crumpled material which she barely discerned with the spot of candle light.

The curtain had had many lives. As it stood right next to the sink, they all used it to wipe their hands. Tsitsi picked up the frail cloth. Silently she withdrew the wire that went through the hemmed top edge of the material, found a spot against the wall to let it rest, then folded the curtain away.

Tsitsi gazed through the open window and listened to the piercing sound of crickets which filled the night air. She dared not trust herself to say anything to Dube. Why was Ponderayi so late? A large calabash burst in the sky and poured streams of liquid into the room. Tsitsi pulled the window to a close.

"It's going to be a big storm," Dube said. "I hope Ponderayi will be home soon." He looked across the high hedge in an attempt to see if there was any sign of Ponderayi among the figures that were already running down the street, holding tightly to their garments.

"He should be here soon. I am worried about the supper which I had not finished preparing before we lost the light." Tsitsi fussed with the pots on the stove.

"Stop worrying about the light. We should have brought in some wood for the stove before the rain started. Perhaps I should go out and get some before it gets too soaked," Dube suggested doubtfully.

"I would rather you didn't. You will be drenched, Father. I don't want to worry about you, too, before Ponderayi comes home. Do you think he is hiding from the storm somewhere? Maybe at the market?"

"I doubt if he would be at the market. Maybe he got off the bus and stayed at the bus station. But maybe the rain caught him when he was already on his way here."

They both stood rooted at the window from where they watched the sky light up in a frenzy. Cruel yellow streaks blazed briefly then disappeared, leaving the echoing reverberations that they felt on the earth where they stood. The street lights sent shimmering sparks of light through the rain, which seemed to explode and break up in many directions.

The rain splashed against the window, clouding their vision. The darkening sky swallowed all shapes. The storm terrified and thrilled them.

"The rain is gone," Tsitsi thought. "It didn't last long."

One of the hinges had also let go and the door slanted pathetically letting in light from the top half.

Ponderayi was standing at the broken kitchen door looking at Tsitsi who was kneeling beside the stove blowing at the embers. Her head drew back several times from the intense heat. She would take a deep breath that puffed her cheeks and then release a forceful breath into the fire. Her face glowed with the heat. Would he manage to tell her?

"How long have you been standing there?" Tsitsi said without turning to look at the door. She had caught his reflection on the shiny surface of the pot.

"Do you have eyes behind your head? How did you know I was here?"

"Shall I tell you a woman's secret? It will no longer be a secret if I do."

"Well . . . I shall not insist. Your hair looks good. Who plaited it for you?"

"I went to the market. Enough of that. Why are you home so late? We expected you sooner. Was it the storm? Your clothes look dry. Is anything the matter?"

"No. Everything is fine. I wanted to . . . I delayed leaving the factory. You know with the bus strike and then the storm . . . I did not want to take a chance." Ponderayi went into the bedroom and said he would change into his old overalls. He called from the bedroom, "Did anyone come asking for me?"

"Why would anyone ask for you? Whom were you expecting?"

"I just thought a couple of boys from work would pass through here. That's all."

"I didn't see anyone, but I went to the market and came back quite late. So maybe someone did come." Tsitsi was throwing another piece of wood into the fire.

"Did father go to bed?"

"He did. He said he has to be up early in the morning to be at work in time."

"I worry about father. He has been acting rather odd. Do you think he will be all right?"

"I think he will be. He is not as odd as you think. He just thinks too much and lets things affect him a little more than he should."

"Do you think he has forgiven me for not going with him to the village to bury his father?"

"Maybe you should have but he has not wanted to discuss any of this with me. He never held it against you. He understood that you could lose your job if you insisted on taking leave after being denied. Why do you talk about it now? It is a long time since it all happened."

"I suppose there is no use talking about it now. Do you need any more wood? I'll get the axe and chop that big log that has been sitting at the back of the house."

"Ponderayi, you don't need to do that. There is plenty of wood that has been cut already. Sit down and have a rest. The food is almost ready."

"I would rather do it. I'll be back in a while." He walked out of the room.

Tsitsi watched him lift the axe onto his shoulder and walk to the other end of the yard. He flung the axe to the ground and disappeared to the back of the house. When he reappeared he dragged a big log behind him. He rested one end of the log on top of another thick piece of wood to elevate its position. The axe swung and landed full force on the log, which splintered into two. Tsitsi heard the familiar sound of breaking wood as Ponderayi divided it into smaller, manageable pieces. He seemed bothered by something, but she had no idea what it was.

"I think you have a big load out there now," he announced when he came back into the room. "May I have a drink?"

She offered him the drink. He looked at her for a long moment. "What is the time?" he asked.

The drink was still in Tsitsi's hands. "The radio said seven-thirty."

It was better that he not accept the drink. If he accepted it, that would be a betrayal, a kind of lie. So he did not take it.

"I have to go for a walk. There is money under the pillow."

He did not wait for her to answer. As he turned to go he saw his father's hat through the open doorway that led to the next room. He picked it up and threw it over his head then went wordlessly out the door.

Whose Baby Is It?

The garbage men came round the streets in a big municipality truck driven by a white man. The children ran outside as soon as they heard it approaching. Because some of them had never been to the city, this was their only chance to see a white man.

The truck would come at great speed and the children jumped up and down in screams of excitement. Three to six men dangling from the rails that were attached to the side of the truck whistled aggressively or sang wild disjointed tunes which they invented as they went along. A lot of the language was not fit for the children's ears. When the truck stopped, briefly, the men jumped off quickly, landing on the ground with a loud threatening sound that sent the kids running back into the safety of their homes, their thumbs pushed into their frightened mouths.

"Woza! Woza! Woza!" The men growled as they picked the huge metal garbage cans and lifted them to their shoulders, rushing to empty them into the yawning truck. The truck would start moving away before the men returned with the bins, so they were always running after it. The metal drums cast behind them, the men leapt onto those rails again, hanging on till the next stop.

The children carefully came out of their hiding places to inspect the new dents on the metal bins thrust so uncaringly to the ground. It was strange and disturbing that if your garbage was already smelling when the men tried to pick it up, they emptied it in front of your yard. The women were left gaping and holding their skirts. When the men had disappeared round the bend the women gathered together and cursed, "Dogs! Dogs! Those are feces-eating dogs!"

It was whispered that the white men gave the garbage workers drugs so they could endure the job and the smelly garbage, which was why they sang and jumped about and did all the crazy things that they were known to do. Some said the workers were all ex-convicts or were recruited from the mental homes. That did not stop the women cursing and saying that even the truck driver was a lunatic who seemed to want to drive over one of the kids. Was he curious to see if a black person bled? There was no doubt he had never passed a test for his licence. He just had it handed to him because he was white. A white man did not need a licence to drive, especially to drive in a black township.

The girl came rushing breathlessly into the kitchen where the mother was bent over the stove preparing the afternoon meal. The girl stood trembling till the mother approached and knelt beside her so that they were the same height. The girl was frightened and stood silently, staring at the mother.

"What scared you so? Did anyone fight with you?" the mother coaxed. The girl started crying. It would be a while before the mother heard what had happened. She was patient, and let the girl cry some more. Then she made her sit down, and held her hand. Black soot floated down from the ceiling, and the water on the wood stove started to boil. The girl looked scared, and the mother started to be afraid.

"They found a baby in the garbage bin, behind the store."

The girl spoke from behind the woman, who turned to face her daughter.

"A baby? How do you know about that?" The mother was anxious.

"The dogs dragged the baby out of the garbage bins behind the store. It looked like a baby so we told some elder women, who came over and chased the dogs away. Whose baby was it, Mother?" the girl asked.

"Are you sure it was a baby?" the mother asked again.

"That is what the women said, and also the police when they arrived. How did the baby get in the garbage bin, Mother?" The girl had many questions, now that she had stopped crying.

The mother took the girl in her arms and held her. How would she purge the fear from her daughter's eyes? It was too soon to think about it. First she must find out what had happened. But she said, "I've told you not to go playing behind the store. Why did you go there?" She needed time to think, not about the baby but about the girl. Did it matter whose baby it had been? The police would find that out soon enough. She had nearly done it herself, when she found herself pregnant and unable to convince the father the child was his. She had had no job, and no way to support a child. The girl must not know what she had thought.

"Do you think the mother is looking for her baby?" the girl asked, looking at her mother inquiringly. She did not understand why her mother was so quiet, or why she seemed so different, so far away. Maybe she was upset with her because she had gone to play at the store. She should not have gone to play behind the store.

"Was the baby dead, Mother? Do you know if the baby was dead?" The girl did not understand it. People talked about dying a lot, about soldiers dying. If you were a soldier you were prepared to die, she thought, but babies were not soldiers, and she doubted that they were prepared to die. Was it possible that the baby was alive?

"What made you cry, my girl? Was the baby hurt?" the mother probed. She wiped the tears off the girl's cheeks, but her face was already dry. The mother's movement made the girl want to cry again and she held back the tears.

"The dogs were dragging the baby, and it was so small, and had no clothes on," the girl explained. A newly born baby, the mother thought, a new life. It grieved her to think of it, but especially to think of her own little girl, whom she was raising alone.

"Do you want to help me cook?" she asked the girl, who shook her head and said she preferred to sit and watch.

After they had eaten and washed the dishes, mother and daughter sat outside on the veranda. People went by behind the hedge, and they watched them pass under the muted yellow glow of the streetlights. Men, coming from the beerhall not too far from the house sang in discordant voices as they went by, staggering to their homes. The mother was glad, for it made the girl laugh and ask if the "poor man" would get home. Women carrying baskets of fish on their heads, which they had tried to sell at the beerhall, also passed by. The mother took the child's hand and cradled it in her own.

The Bordered Road

The river was a dark meandering scar in the distance. Behind my father's hut the large pawpaw tree had fallen. It saddened me to see its roots pointing protestingly to the sky. It had broken open in the middle and revealed a soft fibrous core. Green pawpaws lay all over on the ground, with crooked cracks on their hard shiny exteriors. My sense of loss was not for the juicy yellow fruit that the tree yielded every year. Already I missed acutely those times when I had sat with my back against the thick sturdy trunk to do my sums, read a book or simply bask in the sun. I had climbed the tree carelessly once and the branch had given way. My uncle had shouted, "Girls are not supposed to climb trees!" I landed on a hill of sweet potatoes still clutching the yellow pawpaw that had been my quest. The overripe fruit had splashed against my dress, releasing a myriad round black seeds in transparent watery sacs.

And now, walking towards work, the same sense of wonder and expectancy came over me: the memory of the storm gave me comfort. I would have to walk a little way around the houses in the township before joining the other workers who no doubt would be filling the main road to the city. The bus drivers were on strike today. Earlier I had considered the idea of catching the train to make sure of getting to work on time. However, the day was bright and called one into the streets: it would be a betrayal to get to work early.

The sound of the train reached me as it sped by. It did not seem to have stopped at the local station. Its smoke formed a black cloud which dispersed and left a thin trace in the air. Along the small streets between the houses children were drawing pictures on the wet ground with long sticks. Beside a drainage ditch some boys sat throwing sticks into the running water. After watching in intense concentration, they leapt in unison, each claiming his stick had won the race. They threw in more pieces of wood which they pretended were ships and "discovered" various places. One of them shouted that he had discovered the Victoria Falls as he saw his canoe plunge down over a large log that lay across the running water. The others felt bitter and claimed the textbook at school said that David Livingstone was the only man to have discovered the falls, you had to find something else which no one knew about. The boy felt angry and insisted on his discovery, saying there was nothing wrong with discovering the falls again, he would give them a new name. The others challenged him to tell them the new name but, unable to think of one, he sulked and went home.

A small boy came running from behind a hedge that divided two homes. Another shirtless young boy followed him with a guilty expression on his face. Sap from the hedge had gone into his eyes. The mother, hearing the screaming child called him to the veranda, put him between her knees and squirted milk from her breast into the child's eye. The child protested briefly, ashamed at having this done in front of his friend. The mother cursed him into submission, telling him that he would be blind before he finished his schooling and what then? She was not planning to take care of him when he was an old man.

Voices greeted me as I approached the main road that led into the city. People were standing around wondering what to do. Others were already moving towards the city. Women walked barefoot. The ground was damp and comforting and their handbags bulged where the heels of their shoes jutted. People stood around for a while, talking excitedly about the bus strike and about last night's storm, before beginning to move steadily towards the town.

They planned to follow the wide tarred road into the city. It was a long winding road and on a hot day you could see a tiny lake glittering in the distance but when you moved nearer it disappeared and then you saw it again. Today they would walk along that road, not on it but beside it. People stuck to the edges of the road instead of walking right on it, though it was empty of traffic. They regarded the road with suspicion, as though it represented some larger oppressive thing against which they struggled. The men stuck to one side of the road and the women to the other. The black road divided them, yet kept them together. It was a bitter irony to be on the wayside. Perhaps the road would disappear and stop pushing them to the fringe. Perhaps they would meet in the middle, along a different road.

Children and some adults stood around a truck that lay on the road, overturned by last night's storm. Suspecting that the driver was still trapped inside, people asked questions as they went by.

We had been walking for about an hour. Conversation was becoming less animated as our limbs began to feel the distance. It would be another half hour before we approached the city. I was walking beside a woman who told me she worked as a domestic servant in the white suburbs, on the other side of the city.

"No one will claim to own a bicycle today," she said. "I do not see anyone cycling past," she added as she looked around.

"It is a day for bicycles to rest," I said. My companion responded with a knowing chuckle.

"Maybe something is going to change in this country. Someone will begin to see the folly of suppressing another group."

There was something about the woman's tired voice that gave me confidence: for the first time I felt elation and a sense of release. The sun was coming out and umbrellas burst into the empty sky like flowering plants.

The police and the soldiers arrived suddenly and drove around the crowds to see if there was trouble. The soldiers jumped out of their cars and prodded us with their guns. They asked us to open our bags and scolded us for harbouring big suspicious objects. The men were asked to produce their identification certificates. The jeeps moved behind us, carrying soldiers who pointed loaded guns at our backs, ready to fire.

When we reached the city, the sun sent long shadows to greet us.

Getting a Permit

With her arms crossed delicately on her lap, the Queen of England watches the "permit queue" in the large government office. Part of the queue extends beyond the large wooden doors, and the men lift rolled newspapers over their heads to shield themselves against the blinding sunlight. I have to get back to the radio shop before my lunch hour ends, so I become rather anxious as the clock ticks steadily away before any of the people in front of me are served. The Queen of England smiles at me from her frame on the wall. I look away from the red lipstick smile, but when I look back again the smile has not changed. It is better to avoid looking at the picture at all, but I can still feel those eyes behind my back. A permit to bury my grandfather. Has she ever had to wait in a queue, I wonder. Her dress answers with sparkling jewels resting on intricate embroidery. The Queen of England hangs all day in a permit office on Lobengula Street, staring detachedly. The line moves a little, and my face is reflected in the gold frame that contains the Queen.

An officer comes and stands behind the counter. The men in the queue make their requests for temporary passes. "I've lost my identity," each one says.

"What was your identification number?" the black policeman asks. His voice is impatient, he knows the answer to the question even before he asks it.

"How do you expect to get new identification papers if you do not remember your number? How can we prove you ever held any identity? You want us to start all over again giving you new identity?" His voice is shrill. He pushes his clean shaven face across the counter, aggressively. Several of the men step back.

"If I do not get the identity then I cannot walk around the township. I did not lose the identity. I was robbed."

"Do you know how many times I hear that? I was robbed . . . I was robbed . . . is all I hear all day. None of you people can tell the truth at all. Lies! Lies! Lies!" he bangs the table, then tells the man to wait on the side while he attends to the next person.

The first night after Grandpa died, the men sang loudly throughout the night, leaping into the air and making the ground vibrate. The drummer hugged his instrument between his knees and brought his flat palms down on the taut skin in violent motion. His legs followed the motions of his hands as he raised them with the drum and brought them pounding to the ground. The mbira player sat cross-legged at a corner of the house where there was the least light. The mbira resting between her legs, her palms supported the instrument from below. Only her thumb worked fervently across the bars. She did not look up but played with her eyes tightly closed, her body rocking sadly back and forth, as though she carried a baby on her back that she intended to put to sleep. There was nothing life-denying about her song, though she smiled rather mysteriously under her closed eyelids.

One man beat vigorously on a drum, while the woman accompanied him with yearning sounds from her mbira. The mbira is hard to listen to when there has been a death in the family. The sound of the mbira is like water trickling down a great height, and the regular beating on the small instrument grates against one's heart. It is an instrument that one responds to with the heart rather than the ear. A drum makes you want to get up and dance in rapid motion, a mbira makes you stand still and follow it with a left-and-right or up-and-down swinging of the head. Women who dance to the mbira do so in slow soundless movements, it is not a sound that invites aggression.

A man responded to the drum with remarkable contortions of his

66

body, throwing himself on the ground and rising rapidly to his knees. The crowd moved back and gave him more room. After a while the others started to imitate the actions of the departed as he had been when he lived; the way he walked and spoke. They went into the house and took his clothes, which they wore. Some of those men were good imitators, and everyone laughed freely. The women called the name of the departed and Grandma covered her shoulders with a grey blanket. Nothing had prepared me for the ceremonial fervour of that evening.

As the dancing continued, beer was passed around and everyone drank to speed the night. The mourners intended to be there till morning, sitting around the fire, and talking. Grandma felt happy because everyone had come to console her.

Father had been shattered at the news of Grandpa's death, and the first thing he asked for when he arrived was Grandpa's hat, which I gave to him. Grandpa always wore his hat. Father held the hat lovingly thoughout the evening, as the closest members of the family discussed arrangements for Grandpa's burial. There were four of us in the room.

"We all know Grandpa's wishes," Grandma said, waiting for someone to complete the statement.

"Yes we do. We have to take him home." Father did not look at Grandma as he spoke.

"But we all know the situation is not good for travelling," Grandma had continued, probing the men to make a decision. When Father answered, his eyes remained focused on the ground.

"We have no choice. At least we have to try." He knew this was what Grandma expected to hear, she had already decided it.

"Phineas, you will try to come with us?"

"With us? Are you going to travel with us, Mother?" Father thought his mother too frail to travel.

"Of course. What is the point of it all if I don't come? What shall you do when you get there? Do you know the tradition? Do you know all your father's names by which to call him as you send him to his ancestors? You are an old man now my son, but without the knowledge of your tradition you are only a child with milk on your nose." I was afraid the two would start a quarrel soon. It doesn't take them much to disagree.

"Well then, you shall come. But we should expect anything. We owe this respect to Father. He hated the city. He stayed here only because of his failing health, we must remember that. If he does not rest happy, even we remain cursed in our lives. He will not send us his shadow to guide us through life."

"Phineas, shall you not say anything?" Grandma asked.

"Everything has been said. Tell me what you need me to do. But I will have to see if I can get leave at work to make the trip."

"Has anyone tried to contact Joyce and Sandra to tell them about Father? Do you know where any of them are?" Father asked. Grandma did not like to talk about her other two children. They lived in the middle of the city in a manner that Grandpa had not approved of. Grandma did not even want them to be near her at this time. But she did not get upset or even answer the question. Was it possible she had not heard it? It was decided that I would go to the offices to get a permit for travelling to the country, without which it would be impossible to leave the city.

"That is well. Now we must join the others. I am an old woman and my time will soon be near."

As we came outside we were greeted by the loud singing of the men, and their dancing, which sent thunderous quivers through the ground. One of them led a chant:

You who have gone ahead of us lead the way.

Ewo!

Those who are dead have rested.

Ewo!

We shall follow you in your path.

Ewo!

The night continued in ritual intensity till a soldier arrived to tell us that we had to respect the curfew. Deprived of our company and our rites, we sat in the dark and thought it a bad time to be in mourning.

"What is your problem?" The voice is tight with irritation.

"I need a pass to travel from my work to my home at night. I need the pass to travel during the curfew." It is a woman. She explains that she works in a white neighbourhood and that she has to go home to her children every night because they are alone.

"What about your husband. Why can't you go home the next day?"

"I don't have a husband," she answers without hesitation, it is as though she had been expecting the question.

[handwritten in margin: Is it bec. of state of emergency?]

68

"You just make children on your own? Did your husband leave you because you are a bad woman?" The other men in the room laugh.

"I kicked him out. He was a drunkard," she says, looking the man straight in the eye, as though the comment relates somehow also to him. She seems to be saying, "Either you give me a pass or you refuse, but don't take all day about it."

The policeman stamps her pass and gives it to her. It is only a piece of paper.

It is my turn. I smile blankly at the officer. The man's steely eyes feel as though they would bore a hole into mine but I maintain the gaze and tell my story. The officer smiles as the explanation goes on, until I feel uncomfortable and begin to stumble through the rest of the detail.

"You checked and there are no graveyards around here, they are all full?" the man asks. "You are a complete fool!" He shouts and curses and calls me a liar.

"Do you know there is a war in this country? Do you know that you will get killed if you go into these areas or do you have other motives for travelling?" The man pulls up a chair and sits down.

He talks for a long time and decides that since he has spent so much time on the subject he would look foolish if he doesn't grant the permit. He asks for the death certificate which I have already handed to him. While a copy is being made through a machine at the back of the office, he expands upon the foolishness of my project, but he is now muttering and looking over my shoulder. As he signs my permit he has already begun speaking sharply to the man behind me. He does not appear to hear me thank him, but the Queen of England smiles.

Why Don't You Carve Other Animals

He sits outside the gates of the Africans-Only hospital, making models out of wood. The finished products are on old newspapers on the ground around him. A painter sits to his right, his finished work leaning against the hospital fence behind them. In the dense township, cars screech, crowds flow by, voices rise, and ambulances speed into the emergency unit of the hospital, their flashing orange light giving fair warning to oncoming traffic. Through the elephants he carves, and also the giraffes, with oddly slanting necks, the sculptor brings the jungle to the city. His animals walk on the printed newspaper sheets, but he mourns that they have no life in them. Sometimes in a fit of anger he collects his animals and throws them frenziedly into his cardboard box, desiring not to see their lifeless forms against the chaotic movement of traffic which flows through the hospital gates.

"Do you want that crocodile? It's a good crocodile. Do you want it?" A mother coaxes a little boy who has been crying after his hospital visit. A white bandage is wrapped tightly around his right arm. The boy holds his arm with his other hand, aware of the mother's attention, which makes him draw attention to his temporary deformity. She kneels beside him and looks into his eyes, pleading.

"He had an injection. You know how the children fear the needle," the mother informs the man. She buys the crocodile, and hands it to the boy. The man watches one of his animals go, carried between the little boy's tiny fingers. His animals have no life in them, and the man is tempted to put them back in the box. He wonders if the child will ever see a moving crocodile, surrounded as he is by the barren city, where the only rivers are the tarred roads.

A man in a white coat stands looking at the elephants, and at the man who continues carving. He picks a red elephant, whose tusk is carved along its body, so that it can not raise it. A red elephant? The stranger is perplexed, and amused, and decides to buy the elephant, though it is poorly carved and cannot lift its tusk. He will place it beside the window in his office, where it can look out at the patients in the queue. Why are there no eyes carved on the elephant? Perhaps the paint has covered them up.

The carver suddenly curses.

"What is wrong?" the painter asks.

"Look at the neck of this giraffe."

The painter looks at the giraffe, and the two men explode into uneasy laughter. It is not easy to laugh when one sits so close to the sick. The carver wonders if he has not carved some image of himself, or of some afflicted person who stopped and looked at his breathless animals. He looks at the cardboard box beside him, and decides to place it in the shade away from view.

"Why don't you carve other animals. Like lions and chimpanzees?" the painter asks. "You are always carving giraffes and your only crocodile has been bought!" The painter has had some influence on the work of the carver, lending him the paints to colour his animals. The red elephant was his idea.

"The elephant has ruled the forest for a long time, he is older than the forest, but the giraffe extends his neck and struts above the trees, as though the forest belonged to him. He eats the topmost leaves, while the elephant spends the day rolling in the mud. Do you not find it interesting? This struggle between the elephant and the giraffe, to eat the topmost leaves in the forest?" The ambulances whiz past, into the Emergency unit of the Africans-Only hospital.

The painter thinks briefly, while he puts the final touches on an

72

image of the Victoria Falls which he paints from a memory gathered from newspapers and magazines. He has never seen the Falls. The water must be blue, to give emotion to the picture, he thinks. He has been told that when the water is shown on a map, it has to be blue, and that indeed when there is a lot of it, as in the sea, the water looks like the sky. So he is generous in his depiction, and shocking blue waves cascade unnaturally over the rocky precipice.

"The giraffe walks proudly, majestically, because of the beautiful tapestry that he carries on his back. That is what the struggle is about. Otherwise they are equals, the elephant has his long tusk to reach the leaves and the giraffe has his long neck."

He inserts two lovers at the corner of the picture, their arms around each other as they stare their love into the blue water. He wants to make the water sing to them. So he paints a bird at the top of the painting, hovering over the falls, its beak open in song. He wishes he had painted a dove, instead of this black bird which looks like a crow.

The carver borrows some paint and puts yellow and black spots on the giraffe with the short neck. He has long accepted that he cannot _____ ____ animals, but will not throw them away. Maybe someone, _____ fricans-Only hospital, will seek some cheer in his _____ as finished applying the dots, the paint runs down _____ nal, and it looks a little like a zebra.

_____ er carve a dog or a cat? Something that city people _____ rat would be good, there are lots of rats in the _____ much laughter. The painter realizes that a lot of _____ must be reaching the lovers, so he paints off their _____ umbrella. He notices suddenly that something is _____ ire, so he extends the lovers' free hands, and gives them some yellow ice cream. The picture is now full of life.

"What is the point of carving a dog? Why do you not paint dogs and cats and mice?" The carver has never seen the elephant or the giraffe that he carves so ardently. He picks up a piece of unformed wood. Will it be a giraffe or an elephant? His carving is also his dreaming.

An Unyielding Circle

"Knees! Knees! A woman must bend on her knees to give food to a man. What kind of woman is this?" The woman, not wanting to argue with the drunken men, does as she is told, and the group breaks into applause. When her task is completed, and it is no longer necessary for her to linger, she gathers her skirts from the dust where she has anchored her heavy frame, and detaches herself from the group. Under the market shed, close to where the men are sitting, someone turns on a battery radio and soft lilting music fills the cold afternoon air. As she moves away, the woman beats her arms angrily about her, sending the dust off her skirts.

The men are sitting in a circle passing a calabash of home-brewed beer, and singing loudly. When the calabash is full, its contents lap and spill over, because the men are careless. The ground is dotted with wet patches, and when the men notice, they say they have paid tribute to their ancestors who inhabit the ground. Each picks up the song in different stages, and it is almost as though they are each singing a different song, as their throaty tunes surround the shed. The men's laughter creeps to the subject of women, who abhor this irreverence.

Once in a while the men reach drunkenly into their trouser pockets and contribute towards another calabash, for which they send the youngest member of the group, or call out to one of the women. Their speech is incoherent and they shout loudly to one another, dangling their hands helplessly between their knees. They call to the woman roasting maize cobs, who hurries and hands the beer over, bending her legs briefly to show respect.

Behind the men and slightly over their heads, on a wire that runs round the market shed, crocheted bedcovers and tablecloths are spread like spider's webs. A woman sits on an upturned metal milk-can crocheting a tablecover, shifting her weight in discomfort, and engaging in conversation with the women inside the shed, a distance away from her. But distance does not matter, and she laughs, throwing her head back and lifting her arms up in a gesture that brings a mass of crocheting from her lap into her face. Laughter has brought blinding tears to her eyes and she wipes them off with the back of her arm, reaching into the folds of her dress to hunt for snuff.

Smoke from the maize-cob seller rises and spreads around the shed. The smoke is biting and leaves its victims rubbing their eyes.

"You should make your fire on the other side of the shed, in the direction in which the wind is blowing," MaDube says, without looking up from her mass of crocheting. MaSibanda blows into the fire, then answers.

"How can I roast my cobs behind the shed where nobody is going to see me, away from the customers. Do you think I have come here to play?" She moves some cobs, which rest on a rack from the direct heat of the flames, and settles herself on a goatskin that is laid on one side of the hearth.

"Did they pay you, those men?" MaDube points her crocheting needle threateningly at the group of men, who talk erratically in loud voices.

"I can handle any woman, any woman," a man says, waving his arms drunkenly about, as though some woman has already challenged him. His friends egg him on with loud cheer as though he has spoken for all of them.

"They paid me," her answer is brief, and she looks into her fire, and her maize, seeking an answer there. She feels alone, so completely alone. There will be maize cobs left to take home with her.

"The only way to control a woman is to beat her." Voices reach them, penetrating the quiet they seek. The voices are thick, but not with strength. The women glance at each other, acknowledging the men's intrusion on their calm.

"You have your maize cobs," the woman said, resignedly. "And I have my knitted bedcovers." It sounded simple, matter-of-fact, but the other woman felt salty tears sting her eyes. Why did her friend speak so? Why did she seek to disturb her peace?

"My knitted bedcovers," the woman laughed, and again the crochet rose mockingly to her face. "What can I cover with them?" she asked. "What can I hide with them?" But she heard no answer from her companion. Her fingers and her needles were caught in the holes of her crochet. The men were talking about women they had thrown out of their homes. The men's boasts frightened the women, and they glanced at each other in understanding and sympathy for each other. A flame rose between them, while the men continued their speech. The women, feeling the pressure of the moment, resumed their talk.

"At least you make money, when someone buys your covers. Is that not enough?" MaSibanda asked, raking her coals impatiently.

Enough of raking, who knows how many secrets one will uncover, after a lot of raking in forbidden spaces? She put the raking stick down, but she did not want to look at it, so she put it behind her basket and heard the men shout for more maize.

"Remember to kneel," MaDube mocked her gently. She took the maize to the circle of men, in which she felt like an intruder. She passed the maize, and waited for her payment. She held her arms across her chest, and hoped the men would not find anything to say to her.

"Two hands! Two hands! A woman must use two hands to give food to a man." So they gave her the plate of maize, and she had to start all over again, while the drunken men watched to see that the woman did it right.

"Let her be. Bring the plate over here." The youngest of the men said, sympathetically. But he was defeated by the older men who insisted on seeing tradition expertly and immediately performed, especially if they were paying for their maize. The woman obliged, with a confused and angry heart. When she had performed the men's wishes, they applauded her, and she returned to her place beside the fire. The men sang their old song, and forgot that she had been among them.

The two women sat quietly for a while, but the heavy smoke surrounded them both. The circle of men was hidden from view, though their voices penetrated the dense smoke.

"Do something about your fire, MaSibanda. What kind of wood are you using? What ghosts are you trying to exorcise?" MaDube was rubbing her eyes frantically. The woman blew into the fire vigorously, the logs burst into bright flame, and the smoke thinned out. MaDube lifted her milk can and moved to the other side of the fire, and returned to her crocheting. Her snuff box was caught in the knitting, and so was she. She needed the snuff urgently, after being exposed to the smoke, and the drunken slur of the men who had started singing.

"Caught in a net of crochet," she muttered to her companion. Again she laughed, and the crochet leapt to her face, sympathetically.

"Maize! Maize! Maize!" The men's voices intruded again upon their silence. MaDube rose briskly from her old goatskin and ran to the men, the maize balanced carefully on her plate. She knelt down and used her two hands, then she waited to be paid.

"Sit down! Sit Down! A woman must sit down when she is among men." So she sat down on the bare ground on which beer had been spilled, her hands resting empty on her lap. They counted the pennies, which often fell down and had to be picked up and recounted. For the woman, who was alone, there was nothing to do but wait. She heard nothing, though the men argued endlessly about the sum. She wove a silence that protected and consoled her, postponing the moment when she would have to endure her anguish. Before she could accept the money, the man derided her.

"Two hands! Two hands! A woman must use two hands to receive anything from a man." She did not hear this, but later, she would hate the men and herself. Applauding laughter followed her as she settled, on her old goatskin.

Ancestral Links

They drove through the city in silence, stopping at the traffic lights and watching the people cross the street. Women in high heels looked around at the cars as though not trusting them to stop. A blind man cast his stick back and forth ahead of him, sending those in his path skipping to a safe distance. When he reached the other side of the street, he sat down and extended his cupped hands.

They followed the road that would lead them out of the city. The tall buildings cast long shadows. The street down which they drove was the longest one out of the city, lined on either side with purple jacarandas. They drove under the purple glow which bathed them in warm light. Like a wedding party, they drove under the arch of flowering profusion. Their faces were composed in thick impassive masks.

Fari worried about her grandmother who was sitting alone inside the back of the van. The driver's hands, clutching the steering wheel, were bathed in the purple vibrancy. But maybe it took a careless man to agree to this scheme.

The driver was a man of about forty-five and his dusty brown hair sat in a thick mass that threatened to spill over his forehead. He sat very close to the steering wheel, his short legs reaching out to the pedals.

They passed through a white neighbourhood. The large houses commanded spectacular views of the hills. It was a quiet area, with not a soul in sight. It made you hold your breath, as if you had intruded on some sacred piece of ground, and the driver stepped on the accelerator. Soon they were beyond the neighbourhood and the tarred road turned to dust.

A big sign on the side of the road, announcing that the speed limit was now 80 kilometres per hour, was like a whip to the driver, who sent the car racing ahead in a cloud of dust. They heard sizeable stones hit the sides of the van, and Fari closed the window. Through the dusty window glass the landscape assumed a peculiarly desolate character. With no large trees or bushes, it echoed the stillness of the cloudless sky above. Once in a while a large rock appeared in the distance and when a bird flew out of the empty sky one knew exactly where it would land.

Small shrubs dotted the landscape. The bare red earth was spread out like a blanket to cover some ancestral secret. It was the dry season.

Though they had not spoken, the sounds of their breathing passed involuntary messages between them. It was a test of strength to see who would talk first. Tire sounds broke the quiet in abrasive intrusions where the road became more rocky. A herd of goats crossed the road urged on by a little girl with a large stick that appeared too heavy for her. The driver came to an abrupt stop and a movement was heard at the back of the van. Still, the driver said nothing. He held the skin on his forehead in tight furrows that made you think he was in unbearable pain or anger or perhaps just impatient at the goat that heaved its heavy udder across the road. Would they remain virtual strangers till the end of their journey?

Fari, unable to stand the lack of conversation, cleared her throat to brave a comment. She, too, was impatient. "We are making good progress. We should be there in good time."

"Those who don't hurry also get to where they are going," the driver's answer was brief, but he smiled.

"Pass the bottle of water. It's under your feet. This dust is not a good thing." The woman reached for the bottle, a cooking-oil bottle that still bore its label in bold letters. The driver extended his arm and grasped the neck while keeping his eyes focused on the road. He rested the bottle on his knee and tried to remove the cap.

"Help me with the cap," he mumbled.

"Here. I have got it." Fari felt foolish that she had not thought of doing that before.

"That was good. We should get more of that when we get to a service station."

"I have more water in the bag. And some food too when we feel hungry." She was eager to please and felt glad the air was clear between them, but dust continued to come into the car through the driver's window.

"It is dry in these parts." His face had relaxed and the furrows on his forehead had withdrawn. An outcrop of rock jutted out in the horizon, a solitary landmark in a forlorn place.

"I hope it doesn't rain, because these untarred roads become muddy," the driver said to himself, looking out through the speckled glass as though for reassurance, but the sky gazed dumbly onto the red earth. The car seemed to be the only live thing on the road.

Their first stop was at a police road block, and they waited their turn behind an overloaded bus that seemed to sink between its large wheels. You could tell a rural bus by the sheer amount of dust clinging to its body.

The roof of the bus was loaded with goods of every kind: suitcases, chairs, beds, bags of maize seed, bicycles and chickens in handmade cages. Everyone was asked to vacate the bus for a search and the conductor went up to remove all the items from the roof. Each item had been carefully tied down to the carrier, in intricate knots, for the long journey.

Large drums with black and white stripes had been set up on the road to make sure that no vehicle passed unchecked. The policemen walked around in brown shiny boots that came up to their calves.

Several police jeeps were parked on an embankment along the road. Among the policemen were the soldiers; the police asked for identification, then soldiers searched the goods. The goods were spread out on the ground while men were taken into the forest and asked to strip off their clothing. A woman who held no identification was taken into another part of the forest where she screamed an insult at a soldier. People pretended not to hear. She walked back with her eyes turned to the ground while the soldier prodded her on with his gun. The search seemed to go on endlessly.

Soldiers looked under the seats for weapons and one of them came out carrying a bag which had been left inside, then stood beside the headlights of the bus and shouted loudly for the owner to come and claim it. An old woman emerged from the crowd and pleaded.

"It is mine, my child. . . I left in such a hurry that I forgot."

The black soldier was not about to be mothered.

"Do you have a 'sweet potato' in there?" he asked. He was asking about a hand grenade. "Take your bag and move as far as that tree, then empty it." The old woman did as she was told.

Another soldier climbed down from the top of the bus carrying a large chicken, shouted an insult to catch everyone's attention, then cut off the strings that were tied round the chicken's legs. It started running across the road into the bush but he cocked his gun and shot it. It ran around wildly then fell into the middle of the road. No one moved or responded.

Fari and the driver were watching the scene with interest. It was dangerous to form any judgement of the moment, to predict the result of this encounter. It was better not to attract any attention before their turn came around. They discovered a common desire to communicate. So they resolved to speak in whispers, their lips barely moving and their eyes staring straight ahead.

"I feel thirsty," the driver said.

"I would suggest that we not have anything now. If you are seen drinking something, you will appear too casual."

"Let us wait a while then. Look at that boy, on the left." They saw the boy urinating in his clothes.

"Do you think they will be much longer?"

"I don't think so. They will not find anything. It's just harassment."

The passengers loaded into the bus and the conductor worked at tying the goods on the roof.

"Out! Out of the car and hands up!" The soldier pointed his revolver at the woman and she moved slowly out of the van.

"Identity!" the soldier barked. They dug into their pockets to produce the papers which bore their names and thumb prints.

"Where are you heading?" He looked at them closely, as though they harboured some ill intention.

"Why are you going there?" His eyes still rested on the identification papers.

"To bury my father," Fari said. It was then she noticed that the driver's red shirt and bright yellow trousers were the most inappropriate thing for a funeral procession. She had not thought of these details and had done nothing to take care of them. The soldier stared at the driver and Fari saw the red shirt reflected in the soldier's eyes.

"Do you have a telegram?" the soldier asked. A telegram was the one way to convince a policeman you had reason to travel. Travelling in your own vehicle raised more suspicion than being in a bus.

"We are travelling with the body. It is in the van." Fari and the soldier stared at each other and their eyes wrestled briefly before the man's face exploded into a wide mocking grimace. "Wona! Wona!" He threw his head back and laughed in disbelief, shouting to his friend to come over and witness this madness.

"Are you insane?" he asked, pushing at Fari with the gun, as though she were something dirty and insensible.

"A woman going to the country to bury her father! Do you not have customs where you come from? Why did you not stay in the city and let the men travel? A real township woman, hey?"

His mate arrived. They spoke in whispers for a while then came back to the van.

"Open it! The van. . . Open it!" The second soldier barked.

The driver moved to the back of the car and unlocked the door. Grandmother came out of the car, squinting at the bright daylight and the loud threatening commands.

"Bring it out," the soldier said, covering the men with his gun. When the coffin was on the ground the second soldier commanded, "Open it!"

Fari had not seen Grandfather's face since he had died and she had not wanted to. Now to be forced to see him at gunpoint made her shiver. The driver produced a screwdriver from his pocket and worked steadily to unscrew the lid. When he was finished he got to his feet and looked at the woman who understood the message and knelt down to remove the lid. Though her heart pounded fiercely she took the time to go round the box and block the sun's rays. Grandmother had turned away, unable to witness the desecration. The soldiers searched thoroughly, tapping the sides to check if the box held any secrets.

"We know how you people operate. Using a funeral for subversive movements. You can go now." The humiliation had been complete, but the rest of the car had not been searched.

At the second road block the white soldier asked questions in English, spitting them out in a threatening and superior voice. The black soldier translated them into Shona, his voice replicating the exact authoritative tone and nuance of the white man's voice. When they had answered several questions, the white man left them to the attention of the black soldier. A big van was parked in the middle of the road, to make sure cars knew they had to stop. Other soldiers lounged around in the woods beside the road and gulped down liquids from green metal containers.

"Out of the car," the soldier said. The woman and the driver scrambled out of the car.

"Identification." They produced their papers.

"Where are you going?"

They explained.

"My grandmother is at the back," Fari added, not wanting the soldier to have any surprises. The soldier ordered the driver to open the back door of the van.

"Did you give a lift to anyone?" he asked.

"Hands up! And lie flat on the ground."

They did as they were told then heard the soldier's heavy footsteps as he went round to the back of the van. Fari turned her head sideways as she felt the dust move up her nose but made no attempt to wipe it off, certain that if the soldier saw any unsolicited movement he would shoot. She tried to hold back a strong desire to cough but failed. A ball of dust rose up into her nostrils. Again she resisted the desire to use her hands.

"Out! All of you," the soldier said scrambling into the van. Grandmother stood on the roadside and watched the soldier with interest. He jabbed at the woman and the man and asked if they had already gone through another roadblock.

"We have been searched," the driver said abruptly. The soldier looked down at him suspiciously.

"Show me your travelling permit," he asked, his hand held tightly to his rifle. "Get up!"

"Why do you do this thing?" Grandmother asked.

"What thing?" the man asked curiously.

"Nothing is shameful any more. Not even the dead are respected," she continued. "All we ask is to bury our dead in the manner that we believe, but we are made to feel like criminals. I ask only that you let us go." Fari looked at Grandmother worriedly. There was no point in alienating the soldier further but Grandmother insisted that she had done nothing wrong.

"Stop preaching, old woman," the soldier interrupted. "You women are the last to be trusted. We are only trying to protect you from criminals that are destroying families in this country and you make the job difficult for us. We don't want you to assist them."

The soldier motioned with his gun that they should pass but warned that they should think of stopping in a village somewhere to spend the night because it was getting dark.

"Do you think we should do what the soldier suggested?" Fari asked the driver, tentatively.

"No. I don't think so. We are almost there anyway, and we have not had any trouble." He did not look at her.

"Maybe we should stop," she insisted. The car penetrated the narrow darkness which swallowed them and held them in its womb. The stars appeared to have suddenly multiplied but the mystery that they held in their flashing brightness was a forbidding one. The tree-shadows raced by as the car rumbled into the forest. The moon bled its light onto the front of the car.

As Fari glanced at the driver she realized that some of their newly discovered friendship had gone. The furrowed look had returned to his forehead.

They turned sharply into a narrow road, made another sharp turn to the left, then rattled along a very rough stretch that was not a road but hilly ground that led to a plain. Then they drove into the woods again and rolled through the forest.

The driver, his headlights off, leaned his head towards the windscreen of the van to use as much of the moonlight as was available. He seemed to know his way, because he did not slow down to glance around or check his bearings. When he made another hasty turn Fari gave up hope. Who was this man she had all along simply regarded as the driver?

"Why are we here?"

"Stop asking questions and you will be all right."

Fari was afraid, but she did not know what to ask him.

"You will wait here while I go away. It is in your own interest that you should do as I tell you. I will come back, then I will take you the rest of the way. What I have to do now is very important."

The driver told her to get out while he reached into the car and removed the seats: it was then that she realized they had both been sitting on a cache of ammunition and medicines. She worried about Grandmother to whom she would have to explain everything.

"Whose side are you on?" the driver asked, casually. There was something very decided about the man's voice that made her glance at him sharply, but she failed to discern anything from his face in the dark.

"Why have we stopped?" Fari heard Grandmother ask from inside the van. "Are we there?"

Before she could answer, the driver had picked up his bags and vanished into the night. The woman went into the back of the van and told grandmother that the driver had to go and see some relatives in the next village.

"Why did he stop so far away?" the mother asked.

"Perhaps he did not want the sound of the car to frighten them."

"But to leave us in the forest like this? What kind of behaviour is that? Are you hiding something from me?"

Fari did not know how to break the news gently to her, and Grandmother was already suspecting the truth. "He ran into the bush with a huge bag of arms. Do you realize that we carried those things through two roadblocks?" She trembled to think of the possibility of what might have happened to them. They could have all been shot by the police, on the spot.

"The war is a good war. Do you not support it?" Grandmother asked.

"This is not about supporting the war. This is about risking our lives. I wish father had been able to come, or Tonderayi. It is terrible that both of them were not allowed to take leave."

"We risk our lives every day that we live."

"At least he could have told. How could he use us like that?"

"If you show that you do not trust him, you might not live till tomorrow."

"To meet an ordinary man in the street, to greet him with your hand, to spend the afternoon talking with him and then to discover in the middle of the night that he is not who you think he is–do you not find that disturbing?"

"Would you have helped him if he had told you the truth?"

Fari did not want to discuss the man any further.

"We can only wait for him now. There is nowhere for us to go and I don't think he plans to harm us."

Fari sat leaning against the side of the van while the darkness spread like water across the earth. Tree tops in eerie silhouette flirted with the wind while a string of tiny stars dotted the sky like seeds. Fari lacked the strong sense of tradition that her grandfather had kept despite years of living in the city. His goal had always been to go back to his village. Those who were fighting in the bush were fighting to enter the white man's world, not to preserve their own.

During the Ceasefire

The train, puffing dark clouds of smoke into the morning air, is full of women who are visiting their sons at the assembly camps. Mothers, after years of waiting, are troubled that they may not find their sons. They are anxious to end the long agony; for many years they have been hoping to see their sons return. There are also women who are afraid they will not find their husbands. There are other women too, whose hearts are full of fear, for they have had to survive by finding new husbands; new families have been created. Still, they too are going to the assembly camps, to deal with the past.

Rumours, circulated by interested observers, are rampant that the men in the assembly camps have brought with them wealth–a lot of wealth. The woman has heard these details, and she is going to welcome the troops, and perhaps make a profit.

"Whom are you going to look for?" the older women ask each other. Stories are exchanged and most of them are similar. They hold hands to comfort each other, then they cry to confirm what they have suffered. One brave woman leads a tune, to dispel the sombre mood. It is about Lazarus rising from the dead. When the train stops briefly at a station, the women end the song, and when the train starts, it is not picked up again. "To see my son again . . . to see my son . . . it would be a miracle . . . a miracle . . ." a woman says to no one in particular.

There were hardly any men in the carriage, only the women seeking the lost fruit of their wombs. The young women in the carriage hardly spoke, and looked away shyly from the accusing stares of the older women, who were grieved. The woman looked calmly around her, then abandoned her gaze to the passing trees.

She clutched the fence as she looked into the camp, watching a stream of women register their names, go through the security search, and into the green camouflaging tents spread throughout the expansive fence-enclosed yard. Some women broke into tears as they met their children. Scarred faces that they could hardly recognize turned up from under the sheds and shouted, "Mother! Mother!" But most now bore different names and surnames. They had had to leave the country under false identities, which had soon become familiar. Too much time had passed.

The two camps were located only a short distance from each other. The men had refused to hand over their arms. They wanted to wait for the elections. The woman was going to the fence to wait till someone noticed her. Anyone. The sun formed diamond-shaped shadows on her face. She was scarred by shadow and light. They had arrived in the morning but knew they would have to wait until evening before they were approached. The men in the assembly camps are looking for women. Some have not had women for many years. The bush is a lonely place.

A man came walking cautiously towards her in the early evening and took her into his tent in which women were not allowed to stay overnight.

She was very curious. Had he killed anyone . . . had he killed any white men? What was it like to live in the bush . . . did they sleep at all? But he did not say anything to her. His gaze silenced her. She trembled fearfully and turned her eyes to the green roof of the tent, flapping feebly.

She wanted to ask him if any of his relatives had come to see him. Had his mother come? Was she still living? She wanted to know if he cared. Instead, she lay under the dark side of the tent, and he lay under the muted glow of the setting sun. He did not even touch her for half the night. Then he woke suddenly, his gun in his hand, and asked for her. The woman was indifferent to the gun which the man held lovingly. She doubted he would give her anything. She would try her luck with someone else tomorrow. She heard a rumbling through the soft ground. As the soldier entered her, his gun cradled tenderly under his right arm, she wondered if it would rain. He did not circle her with his arms. The woman was concerned about the halo that she saw light up over the man's head, beneath the tent's roof.

The sky lit up with exploding fire. The two assembly camps were in dispute. The night erupted into gun song.

As fire landed next to the tent in the middle of the night, the woman regretted her visit. The man had abandoned her wordlessly, leaping out of the cavelike space he had tried to humanize with a female.

The woman lay still, feeling the cold empty space beside her, where the man had lain. She watched the light increase over the tent, and wondered if the soldier would survive. After putting her clothes on, she lay down again, and waited.

Then the troops arrived in both camps, their lights burning large circles on the sides of the tents, and told the women who were cowering under the sheds to get into the large vans. The windows of the vans were fortified with gridlike bars, and the woman felt caged. Her eyes followed an arc of retreating fire. She felt a salty trickle reach the edge of her mouth, and wiped her tears with the back of her bare arm.

The women spent the night in a prison cell, and were released in the morning, thrown into the streets. The fighting in the camps continued. During the Ceasefire.

Some men died, only a few weeks after they had returned home, and after years of escaping enemy fire in the bush. The woman got on the train to go back home and in the distance, at the assembly camps that had held her hope the day before, the sky again reverberated with machine gun fire. The woman was startled to hear the train let off a piercing scream, into the night sky. Her moment had come and gone.

It Is Over

It was obvious that the train would be at the station for a while before moving on to the city. The guard had disembarked and was walking the length of the carriages. Chido stood outside a while before getting on, and watched a young black man wearing a blue Rhodesia Railways uniform shovel coal into the furnace. His strong arms heaved back and forth, with his lips held in a tight grimace, fighting the searing blast. He sweated profusely. Chido felt the cold air on her cheeks, and held the scarf tightly around her neck.

A grating sound penetrated the chilly air each time the man pushed his shovel into the pile of black coal. It was against this too that his contorted face protested. A cloud of black dust escaped the imposing pile of coal and sought his face, and the man coughed loudly, putting the shovel aside to hold his chest. He wiped his arms, which were covered with soot, but the black dust clung to them. Meanwhile, the coals blazed an angry red.

Realizing there would be a lengthy delay, the passengers on the train took the chance to get out of the train and walk about. Men urinated into the long grass. The women, with babies suspended in thin cloth along their backs, found patches of bare earth between the grasses, where the men would not see them.

Chido felt alone among the many figures that walked up and down the length of the train, shouting greetings. The cold air stood between them. The morning she had arrived home from the war, Mother had not recognized her. She had stood wordlessly on the stoop and stared at Mother, who stared back blankly. Then Chido had spoken, and through her daughter's voice Mother had remembered. That morning Mother had cut bread for her and made some tea, warming the water with the only wood she had left. After the embraces and the ululations, the mother prepared the daughter for a new beginning. Father had died and Mother was now on her own. Mother complained that Chido's brother Peter, who worked at the radio shop and was now married, hardly gave her anything to help her survive.

"Chido, what are you going to do, now that you have come back?" That morning Chido did not answer, but moved into her old room to rest.

On the second morning after she arrived, Chido sat with Mother under the shade of the veranda, watching people's heads go by over the high hedge.

"How was it there where you were?" Mother asked, apprehensively. Chido was angry that she should ask such a question, that she should expect an answer from her.

"It was all right," she said, shrugging her shoulders impatiently. "It was all right." Mother knew that her daughter was impatient. Still, she was curious.

"Were you afraid, my child? I worried so much about you. I used to dream . . ." But Chido felt that Mother was shifting another burden onto her, and she did not want to listen.

"Don't talk like that, Mother. Don't talk like that." The daughter was aggrieved. She did not want to remember. Talking made her remember. She did not know who she had become, and she did not want to find out. Why did Mother want to find her out?

"Why do you hide from me?" Mother pleaded. "I am your mother." Chido looked away, at the pink blossoms covering the peach tree, which were very pretty in the sun. When the wind blew, some of them fell. Mother looked at the stranger who was her daughter, and moved nearer to her, seeking to recognize her. This the daughter hated, but she could not move away, in case she hurt the mother. She hoped Mother would not touch her, and she felt very angry and confused.

"Chido. What will you do now that you have returned?" Mother asked again. It was only two days since she had come home, and Chido did not want to answer the question.

"The girls you left behind are all married now and have children. You should visit Maria, your friend from high school. She always asked about you, when you were away. Do you not want to see Maria, and her children?" Mother asked, but she did not put her arms around the girl, and Chido was glad for it.

"I will see Maria, Mother, but not today."

"What kind of job are you going to get, since you did not finish your education? Maria is now a school teacher. She has done very well." Mother did not know how much she hurt her daughter. "Now that the war is over, and Independence is here, Maria says she is going to be teaching in the city, with the white teachers."

Chido did not deny that she had been left behind. Those who stayed at home had more success. The kind of success that counts.

"You should be thinking of getting married," Mother said. "At least that will be a beginning." Mother was confident that she was right, but the girl knew that she was being told to leave, soon after she had returned. The girl knew that she was a burden on Mother, who did not have the means to shelter her.

On the third day after the girl had returned, she sat with Mother in the kitchen, and told her that she was leaving.

"Where are you going?" Mother asked with panic, though she felt glad that a decision had been arrived at.

"I am not sure yet, but I will leave tomorrow."

"You have not seen your brother Peter. Do you not want to see him? Maybe you will need him one day, so try and part on good terms. You have also not met his wife. Do you not want to meet your brother's wife?" Mother's effort to keep the family together would not succeed. This was the second time the daughter would be leaving home, but this time the decision was not entirely hers. She had nothing that she could claim as her own.

"How will that help me, Mother? How will that help me?" the girl pleaded powerlessly. But Mother was ignorant of the girl's fears, and insisted.

"It is over, Mother," the girl said, walking out of the doorway. "It is over." But Mother only looked through the window at the rain which had stopped falling. Chido left for the train station, on her way to Harare, to try life in a large city.

The guard blew the whistle, and the passengers scrambled into the carriages. Chido was one of the last to get into the train, and she watched the trees speed by, and the smoke from the train greet the clouded sky.